To Josuchina + Goffie
I hope you enjoy
the record

Alan
March 2008

Death of a Nightingale

Inclusion or Disillusion? and Other Heresies

by
Alan Share

authorHOUSE®

AuthorHouse™ UK Ltd.
500 Avebury Boulevard
Central Milton Keynes, MK9 2BE
www.authorhouse.co.uk
Phone: 08001974150

This book is a work of fiction. People, places, events, and situations
are the product of the author's imagination. Any resemblance to actual
persons, living or dead, or historical events, is purely coincidental.

First published by AuthorHouse 1/8/2008

ISBN: 978-1-4343-5179-1 (sc)
ISBN: 978-1-4343-5861-5 (hc)

Printed in the United States of America
Bloomington, Indiana

This book is printed on acid-free paper.

In Memory of my mother, Esther

*When you meet your friend on the roadside or in the market place,
let your spirit in you move your lips and direct your tongue.
Let the voice within your voice speak to the ear of his ear.
For his soul will keep the truth of your heart as the taste of the
wine is remembered
When the colour is forgotten and the vessel is no more.*

The Prophet - Kahlil Gibran

Preface

Back in 1988 I was a local business man, and a member of my local Rotary Club. I was persuaded, as an act of Rotary service, to become a Governor of a Special School for physically disabled children with an associated learning difficulty. A year later I became its Chair of Governors, a position I held until 2002.

This was to change my life and apart from anything else, help to turn me into something of a writer - a very great surprise that I did not expect.

At Merton College, Oxford, I had planned to become a barrister, and to the extent that once a barrister always a barrister, I still am. My career at the Bar in Manchester was to last for only three years. Manchester came and went.

I was won over by Jo Grimond's inspirational leadership of the Liberal Party, and I moved from the Bar to the Head Office of the Party in Victoria Street, London, as Executive Assistant to its Secretary. In those days the Government, as Jo Grimond once chided it, "couldn't run a sweetie shop in the Lothian Road". Would they manage it any better today? Some things have not changed very much over the years. Therein lies a part of the problem. Anyway, I worked there for three years before joining a family furniture company. I had tried to avoid that but, as it turned out, I was to enjoy the ride, and stay with it until I retired. So far as the Liberal Party was concerned, I had walked with Jo Grimond "towards the sound of gunfire", but I never quite got there - nor, I fear, did he.

It is amazing how you can misread things when you are young.

I don't, however, begrudge either of my early short lived work experiences. Both of them were learning experiences. Building bricks, I call them.

On the Northern Circuit I was privileged to have as Head of Chambers, and as my pupil master, the late C.N.Glidewell, CNG to everyone who knew him. He was a man with old fashioned integrity. He was also a master of advocacy - particularly good when he showed up the ineptitude of local planners. He also had style. All of this was somehow encapsulated in his choice of car - a *Bristol* - a prestigious saloon engineered with traditional British quality in its design. In all ways CNG was a cut above the ordinary.

The Law taught me the importance of two things. Firstly keep everything in writing. I have paid a heavy price for that. And secondly keep as far away from lawyers as possible. I have not always been successful in this, and sadly have found that a few can best be described as little more than gas meters constantly demanding to be fed. Not all merit that description, and I do exempt my own solicitor here.

My experience of politics encouraged me to keep as far away as possible from that too. But this has never been an easy thing for me to do.

Becoming a Governor was the start of my serious writing - a diary to keep a written record of everything. Letters, memoranda, and emails, you name it, I wrote them, and copied them into my diary.

I must record one other youthful mistake. I used to imagine that the world was a rational place. My wife, who had studied Psychology at Newcastle University, put me right. I suddenly realised that reasoning usually starts in the gut, not in the brain. At Oxford, Roman Law, not Psychology, had been an important part of my course in Jurisprudence. A pity since this revelation has changed my way of thinking - and of writing ever since.

It has influenced the way that I have processed many words in the last twenty years.

Allow me to explain. Over a hundred special schools have been closed in recent years as successive governments moved more and more children with special needs into mainstream schools. The buzz word here is 'Inclusion¹'. Although the school I was associated with is still in existence as I write this, its future has been uncertain for many years. Parents who fought to keep it open have been swimming against a strongly running tide that constantly threatened to engulf it.

This is a great shame because it was a very good school, and it certainly wasn't cut off from the outside world. This was not just my view of it - OFSTED was of the same opinion.[1]

I still have snapshots of the school in my mind from the time I joined it as Governor in 1988. A head teacher with a vision and a mission statement shared with his deputy *"Whole School - Whole Child"*, warm, dedicated and committed staff, and above all bright eyed, happy purposeful children, enjoying their school days and helping each other along the way. A win, win situation for everyone included in it - parents, teachers, carers and most of all its pupils. Presentation Evenings captured it all. That is where they all came together in one joyous, celebratory event.

They all had the pride of achievement - without being proud. In my gut I felt that to close this school would be a real error of judgment.

It is in this context that I write this book. I must stress that it is a piece of fiction. I dedicate it to all those people working with special needs, to children with special needs and to their parents. I came to have a huge respect for all of them. In their interests I would like to combat the stigma that moves towards Inclusion have, at times, wrongly attached to special schools. This is important since the tide towards a policy that was based upon the dogma of Inclusion, and not upon its practicability and its suitability, may now be on the turn.

I sense a growing awareness that inclusive education is not appropriate for all children with special education needs.[3]

Contents

Prologue

We shall not cease from exploration
And the end of all our exploring
Will be to arrive where we started
And know the place for the first time.

TS Elliot, Four Quartets, Little Gidding 1942

I believe in a Creator, though many do not. But I cannot see some great figure sitting astride the Universe with all its galaxies determining everything, and I cannot see someone that I can personally talk to. So I can live with ritual; but prayer is more difficult. I am envious of Emma Kirk, the music teacher in the play, who has that facility. When she finally meets her Maker, she will do so with equanimity. I hope you will warm to her as I do.

My route to my Creator is through my relationship with man, and with an awesome awareness of the incredible wonders of the Universe, of which man is but a tiny part. For me God does not replicate the attributes of man. That would deny us our freewill. And we would all be puppets on his string. Whether we are believers or non-believers we must surely not be puppets.

There is a price to be paid for that. For good or for ill, we have a choice. We can be saints or sinners, and there has never been a shortage of either. Starting way back in the Garden of Eden - or just in the distant past - we were given personal choice in our lives as our birthright. This is one of the things this book is about. How we exercise it, and how much of it we are actually allowed to exercise in the 21st Century. If you see personal choice as a bourgeois fad, you cancel out personal responsibility too, and herald authoritarianism. Is that what you want?

Fate steps in

Despite all that I think that some things have to happen. Providence takes a hand. This Prologue was the result.

Consider the following coincidence and its consequences. I am in Manhattan for a number of reasons. One is to see old friends, not least to see a beautiful lady, now in her nineties. I met her almost fifty years ago when she welcomed me to her home as a guest of her somewhat eccentric son. He must have been more than a bit eccentric. He wrote from New York offering his services to the British Liberal Party. I was also a bit eccentric at the time. I was working in Victoria Street, and I replied to his letter, asking him to call in. This was the start of many treasured trans-Atlantic friendships that I have come to enjoy.

The other reason I am in New York is to look at works of art. I have seized a rare opportunity to look in wonder at Gustav Klimt's Adele Block-Bauer I at the Neu Galerie, and I am in a café enjoying a cup of coffee. I notice at the next table a short, stocky, bespectacled, well dressed but somewhat crumpled very senior citizen. What took my eye was that he was tucking in to a large piece of chocolate cake, a huge mound of cream, and an ice cream sundae. He was also sporting four colourful badges on his dark professional suit as well as a very lively tie and something else, which I cannot make out, dangling round his neck. This was not an everyday occurrence, even in New York.

We got into conversation and I discovered he was a retired doctor and a wise, interesting and probably lonely old bird. He had a very dry sense of humour that I warmed to. As he drew upon his reservoir of quip and anecdote, his serious face melted into a smile that was both benign and mischievous, a true raconteur. He was also a flirt with the ladies. We invited him to join us that evening for a meal, and to our great pleasure he did. I thought it would be lovely to introduce this great character to my American hostess of yesteryear. It was an idea that appeared to die a death.

Quite a few days later I was walking through Central Park on my way to see my ninety year old lady friend. As I walked down Park Avenue, who should I see but the same crumpled up character clutching a paper parcel in one hand and a broken down walking stick in the other emerging from an apartment. A moment earlier, a moment later, I would have missed him. I invited him to come with me. And so we walked at something less than a snail's pace to our destination, stopping only to enable him to talk to every doorman en route, reminding them of his former patients in that particular apartment block, and to catch his breath.

As we walked we discussed many things. His father had been one of the founders of the American Liberal Party. I didn't know that one existed. I shared with him my view as to the Achilles heel of the Liberal - naiveté. An endearing quality if you recognise it, a very dangerous one if you don't. "Insanity," he said. He reminded me of King Lear. We were on the same wavelength.

When we reached my friend's apartment, we discussed the play and the background to it, and I read out a few extracts. She had already read most of it. She said that she liked it, but that from time to time it had lost its way. At this point my newly found friend and admirer urged me to consider the methodology of George Bernard Shaw, write a Prologue and put into it the generalities of the thoughts provoked in me by my writing. I could then leave them out of the play almost altogether. This actually tied in with some other helpful advice from another quarter. This friend had identified parts of my writing as "rant". She had liked the rest.

"Rant", of course, is a word some people use to dismiss thoughts and ideas that they cannot go along with. But she was right. I needed another seedbed for them. A Prologue suddenly made sense to help my readers on their way.

If you want to understand the writing, you need to have some understanding of the writer, and where the writing comes from. I am interested in the microcosm, and I am interested in the whole which the microcosm reflects.

So here are the thoughts behind the play. The bee - or bees - in my bonnet that refuse to fly away. The assumptions, I suggest, that shouldn't always be assumed, that I invite you to question. A play focussing on a school for children with Special Educational Needs provides me with a vehicle in which to travel the world. Come and join me on my journey.

The play is set in a special school. So, firstly, here are my thoughts about Special Educational Needs, about the policy of Inclusion in Education[2] and about the right to it. Just why, despite all the paper plans, despite all the talk of human rights, why do they continue to get it wrong? Why do they fail to give so many children the one chance they have?

Inclusion or disillusion?

Rights! My mind goes back to a lecture by Herbert Hart, the eminent Professor of Jurisprudence at Oxford.[2] He explained that there was not one single meaning for the word "right". There could be five or more different meanings depending on how it was used. In addition "rights" are not always complementary to each other and they are rarely, if ever, absolute.

Sometimes one person's "right" - say a UK citizen's right to live in safety and not to be blown up by a propane gas bomb loaded with nails - or to have a fear of this - may conflict with the rights of migrants seeking to enter this country. You have to be very careful how you use the word "right". You need fine judgment and, as Professor Hart argued, a sense of fair play in deciding when and how to assert it. It is just as well to remember that while human rights may enable lawyers pronouncing on them to enjoy the fruits of Utopia; they allow the rest of us only a partial glimpse of it. In Professor Hart's own words human rights are "the prime philosophical inspiration of political and social reform".[4] Often they are no more than that.

So, when you talk about the "right" to Inclusive Education you should recognise that some will want to assert it and may succeed and thrive. Some may assert it but be disappointed and wish they hadn't. Some may want to assert it but be denied it. Finally, some may not want to assert it at all but be forced to accept it with no other realistic choice available, and some may want to assert a different right altogether - the right to go to a special school. Remember that children without special needs have their rights too. This actually summarises how things are.[5]

Social reformers have not always grasped this. I fully appreciate that an international consensus set the wheels in motion, but I suspect that many have looked at this simplistically, seeing it as essentially society's difficulty not an individual's and, with the very best of intentions, projecting what they *felt in their gut* they would want for *themselves* for everyone else, a not uncommon mistake. Even disability organisations that have done so much to help the disabled may have fallen into the same trap. That is why they may not always have seen the quite different and varying needs that some children and their parents actually have, and a not always pleasant reality they have to deal with every single day. Very simply, some do not want an open door. What they want is a helping hand and the comfort zone of their own company. For them change is a worry and a threat.

4

Inclusion is a concept that is absolutely wonderful in the libraries of the mind. It is not always quite so wonderful in the classrooms of the real world, especially if vulnerable children are excluded when they are supposed to be included, made to feel unwanted and, at its worst, shoehorned into a hostile environment.

Today classrooms are populated by far too many bully boys and girls.[6] Teachers may have too little time and sometimes too little training as well. Supply teachers are here today and gone tomorrow. Teaching assistants don't always know how to stretch children in the way that trained teachers do and, in many cases, do not improve attainment. Ironically they can create a sense of exclusion in an inclusive environment, stigmatising pupils in the process. Teachers are not always trained to relate to them. A hundred thousand more teaching assistants have come on stream since 1997, quite a number of them supporting children with special needs[7]. Did anyone anticipate this - and calculate the cost? In addition, there are too few therapists and money is still short. But then the policy of Inclusion was never properly costed by anyone in the first place.[8] Thus, cost benefit analysis is a totally alien concept.

It is far too simplistic and naïve, to say that the failure of the plans can be attributed to the shortage of money. If that is the case, then in the nature of things they will be destined always to fail. Fortunately there is more hope than that if people realise it. This is not just about money. It is about *the way* that money is spent, *who* spends it, and *where* it is spent. You don't solve problems simply by throwing money at them. The very first thing you have to do is to try to understand the problems.

What I sense children with special needs and their parents want is not sympathy but understanding and compassion. You express sympathy, but you feel compassion, a very important distinction.

This is another reason why well-intentioned plans have failed. Compassion can never be part of the job description of civil servants. Even empathy may be too much to ask. Central government is too remote, and local government is too parsimonious. Neither is best structured to deal with something that would better be handled by authorities that are regional and accountable. Airports are managed in this way.

Just how sensitive is the system today to individual needs that are far more numerous and varied than most people realise? Does it even begin to think in terms of a holistic approach to learning difficulties? I pose these questions.

Education should be about preparing children to be included in society as adults. One form of education does not fit all children, and it is very unwise to believe that it does.

Therefore I present *Death of a Nightingale*. In the play the headteacher, Margaret Williamson, comments *"Your social engineer has put square pegs into round holes ... with Araldite."* He does so whenever he goes against the grain of man's natural instincts, and because his focus is on outcomes, and not on meeting individual needs. He does not always know what those needs are, nor does he feel any need to know. He combines myopia with tunnel vision. Society then has to cope with the consequences. This, however, is just square one.

Where does control stop and participation begin?

Many teachers are highly committed to their job, but they have too many things asked of them that get in the way, and not enough time and energy to do it all. Then there are all those working in the public service who feel obliged to do some things they know they shouldn't be doing, or not do things that they should. There are school governors, and people like them, who are doing valuable voluntary work within the community, but who are deliberately denied the tools to do it properly by those who prefer to do it themselves, but want to make it look otherwise.

It is the System that needs looking at, the con in consultation, the charade of partnership, the make-believe, and as a result, the mess of much of it.

I am only saying here what more and more people are saying. Lying has become endemic from the top downwards. But, when proven lying is a heinous crime in our society. the denial and the cover-up necessarily follow, and compound the initial problem. The checks and balances that I always thought were an integral part of a democratic society have been disabled. If there is a cock-up, heads should just occasionally roll. They do in the private sector.

In 2006 The Institute for Public Policy Research issued a publication entitled *Whitehall's Black Box: Accountability and Performance in the Senior Civil Service*. Here is one quotation from it. "What, then, is precisely wrong with the way Whitehall is governed? This is best put by saying that lines of accountability are weak and confused. There is a 'governance vacuum' at the heart of Whitehall."

I pose the question in the context of education for special needs. Is the system of government providing an education that enables children to rise to the challenges of the 21st Century? It needs to look at itself in the mirror. Read Rudi Giuliani's book entitled *Leadership*.⁹ This is what he says about education in New York City: "What the system *should* have been about was educating its million children as well as possible. Instead it existed to provide jobs for the people who worked in it, and to preserve those lobs regardless of performance." Could the criticism apply to this country as well?

The recent *Power Report* ¹⁰ pointed to "the weakening of effective dialogue between governed and governors" and "the rise of quiet authoritarianism within government." If I can remove the wrapping paper, it is saying that our democracy is often just a sham, and that the problem is not so much spin as twist. It is a serious criticism of those who wield power - the subtle and not so subtle pressures they exercise - the patronage they use to get their way. It should be no surprise that lawyers, accountants, academics and others, from time to time compromise strict standards of professional behaviour and play word games instead. I have seen it happen. If the System does look itself in the mirror, it needs to recognise that the mirror itself is a distorting one. Will it do even that? Sad to say, the report has already been allowed to gather dust as reports of this kind invariably do, and everything goes on as before.

Like everyone else I have been an observer. What I have seen in one small part of Britain is, I suspect, a microcosm of the whole. What I have seen could happen anywhere, at any time. All of that is now ancient history for me. What I write here is fiction from first to last, but it is born of the experiences and of the paranoia of things that I have seen. And I write it as a tragedy, which I believe it is. I hope that I do not give too much away if I say that there are no individual heroes or heroines in the play, no individual villains either. All the characters are in one way or another victims or casualties of a system that has somehow lost its way. They're all human. If there is a hero, it is Brighouse School itself.

Thoughts about music, art, literature and God

All is not bad. There are opportunities as never before for those who can seize them. And pleasures abound for those who can afford them, or have been shown where to look for them. The world is a big and exciting place for those who can find their way around it. And as I have thought myself into the characters of Emma Kirk and Joan Errington, the Music and English teachers that I have created, both with a real sense of vocation, I have felt things about Music and English that I was not aware of before. And I have thought more about God, especially in relation to the spiritual side of Music. I have been thinking about a Universal Creator through the prism of Music. They have, after all, been travelling companions since the dawn of civilisation.

Music is good for the soul. Whether playing or just listening, it is something you should learn at school. As Anthony Storr illustrated in his book *Music and the Mind* it can have a special value for children with learning difficulties.'' I am indebted to my music teacher who played records to us with, as I recall it, fibre tipped needles. Once learned at school, it will last a lifetime. It has for me. With great Music like great Art you can touch eternity. These are moments that will last for ever.

English, well English we take for granted, but we shouldn't. It is England's enormous gift to the world, enabling it to talk to itself. If offers its rich vocabulary and strange punctuation, which I can never seem to get absolutely right because I was never properly taught it in the first place. And it offers its great literature. But then I am sure that the Romans didn't appreciate what a wonderful gift Latin of all languages was going to be to the world either.

What a legacy England has bequeathed with Shakespeare and Milton, with Wordsworth and Rupert Brooke, and with all the wonderful writers of today and yesterday. We have to make sure that their legacy is not lost along the way. Our schools also have to make sure that the children of those who have recently arrived at our shores are given every opportunity to see, hear, use and enjoy this legacy to the full. That is a major task in its own right, one of many they have, apart from meeting special educational needs.

And where does the inspiration come from for art, music and literature? Can it simply be explained by the laws of evolution? I'm not so sure. I shall return to this.

Thoughts about politics

For many years I went along with the idea, as I guess most people do, that 'Liberty, Equality and Fraternity' were, and are, worth going to the barricades for. But is it?

'Liberty', too often today confused with License, is in today's complex world constrained by rules and regulations. We are moving towards an Orwellian State with cameras everywhere, computers that can read your every movement and censor your email, with DNA profiling and, as I write, with an ID card to come. This is a new world. Are you really free when you are intimidated, bullied or cajoled into doing things you shouldn't do or into not doing things you know you should? The play shows how easily this can happen today, and the consequences, when the abiding rule is ' to know your place'. But if Liberty is simply an absence of slavery or torture, is that really enough? It certainly was around the year 1800, but what about today?

'Equality' - who really does want Equality? Only those painfully less equal or those who do not always practice what they preach. Not an argument for not wanting a fairer society, a fairer world and equality of opportunity. But 'Equality'? Is that the right word? Is it the right word in education? Is it the right word in health? Wouldn't the word 'Equity' be a far more realistic and an altogether better mantra? Deep down in Britain fairness and fair play are the words that really resonate, and make the country a good place to live in.

And 'Fraternity'? Some hope if you think about war and conflict over the years and to this day, right around the globe. Just how much 'fraternity' is there in our schools when, according to *Mencap*, eight out of ten children with learning disabilities are bullied, with some probably scarred for life?

In short, today Liberty is absolutely impossible to define. Equality is absolutely impossible to achieve, and Fraternity is simply impossible. What about Integrity, Diversity, Harmony, Accountability, and common decency? What about old fashioned Trust? None of these were ever listed. A bit of competence would help too, and a bit of wonder. We are driving blind. No wonder there are errors of judgment.

And here is another blind spot. Personal satisfaction sits alongside financial reward as a basic human need. That is why self-fulfilment and self esteem make a major contribution to personal happiness irrespective of income. Are they rated as important in the corridors of power? Specifically, are they rated as important in the Department for Education and Skills (DfES) and in Local Education Authorities (LEAs)? They should be. Life is not just about money and an opportunity to spend it. With today's excesses of drugs, drink, gambling and promiscuity, all increasingly off limit, happiness, especially in the young, is increasingly elusive. This should surprise no-one. It's what happens when you confuse liberty and licence, imagining that you are providing the one, when all you are doing is encouraging the other. It's what happens when pride is at a premium, when pills appear the best answer.[12]

The highest common factor – Humanity?

In our troubled world we need an altogether new and simpler banner to say it all.

It should simply read 'Humanity'. In our newly discovered *global* world, this should now be the focal point of our aspirations, the spark to our idealism, the Litmus test for all human behaviour. It should be a marker post in the quest for peace, and against all forms of prejudice and discrimination.

Some people are there already - *Médecins Sans Frontières*[13]for instance and the thousands and thousands of people who do unsung, voluntary work quietly. There is also the army of those who care for their patients, or for their family, neighbours and friends. But still not nearly enough people rally behind the banner of 'Humanity', not least those best positioned to assert it in government, on a pulpit or in multinational companies. There its value is understated and at times undervalued in the pursuit of other things. Power over people can be a terrible responsibility. Shame on all those wielding it, if they abuse it!

Shouldn't we be defining what is humane and promoting it? Defining what is inhumane and condemning it? Shouldn't we try to identify who respects human life on this planet and who threatens it? Shouldn't we look within ourselves for compassion for those less fortunate than ourselves - children with special educational needs for example, and their parents? It is of the essence, yet sometimes we do these things, but sometimes we don't.

This does not divide people by race or by religion, by political persuasion or by gender. Yes, men and women are wired up differently, and one shouldn't assume otherwise, but they derive their energy from the same power source.

Asserting our common humanity distinguishes between fundamentalism that can be all right if it is simply a personal belief, but may well not be okay if it is fanatical, and impacts on those who do not share it. It distinguishes between dogma, which can also be all right, and bigotry which is not. It distinguishes between those who care about future generations on this planet and those who are motivated simply by avarice for money or for power or both. It divides between people who are basically humane and those who are basically inhumane. It's as simple as that. Sadly, not everyone that is human is humane.

And even in war, when the guns are firing, and when bombs and rockets are exploding, those who think that this has no relevance make a big mistake. Then it is just more difficult to define, and harder to achieve. The imperative however remains to help create the peace afterwards.

And we should stop thinking that when you are confronted by evil you have only a two-way choice, between appeasing it and confronting it. Appeasing it is an act of weakness that accepts it. Confronting it militarily can sometimes be an ultimate necessity, but sometimes is an act of lunacy, that feeds evil, by giving it the oxygen of publicity and a challenge that it actually relishes.

The third option is containment, an act of quiet strength. Quarantine the monster until it self destructs - until it dies of its own poison. We have seen this work with the rulers in the Kremlin and with Mao Tse Tung. Bad notions can no longer compete for long in our global world. Let them try, and then eventually fail. They will implode. Let people realise that just as Communism does not work, so other dogmas and ideologies have their fault lines too. That is how we should be dealing with religious fanaticism.

True faith and real doubt – room for both?

There is not much further to go now, as I share my thoughts with you. Stay with this just a little while longer! If I think about 'Humanity' I have been thinking too about God. Religion and faith both come into the play. The music teacher in the play, Emma Kirk, is a Pentecostal Christian. She lives her faith, and she makes it her own. She breaks the rules and talks about it in the classroom. Terry, a pupil, expresses the doubts of his father, an atheist. Another parent, Anwar Fawzi, a taxi driver is a Sikh. The English teacher, Joan Errington, is agnostic. The spirit of music carries a message to all of them.

I should tell you where I stand. I am a member of one of the smaller Jewish communities in the UK. I have an approach to my religion that is my own.

Along with about half of the world's population, I believe that there is a Creator. I sense that many, many people feel an enormous inborn need of a faith, a roadmap for this life and a passport to the next. At its best, for those who believe, faith is a wondrous gift from Heaven.

It explains the beginning and the end of existence. It helps people to live with themselves, and to seek forgiveness when they need it. With its ritual it provides constancy and a colour to communal identity. It is the source of solace and strength in the face of adversity; it provides a basis for compassion, reconciliation and healing, and it gives a set of values to live by. I think of people like Mother Teresa[14] Archbishop Desmond Tutu[15] Rev. Martin Luther King Jnr[16] Mahatma Ghandi[17] and His Holiness the 14th Dalai Lama, Tenzin Gyatso [18]. It is about birth, marriage and death, pain and guilt, and about loyalty to the tribe.

One of my closest friends is an atheist. That is his deeply held personal conviction, and there are many others who share it with him. He asserts that his values are at the very least as worthy as those founded upon a religious belief, and he reminds me of the blood that has been shed over the centuries, and to this day, with all the wild frenzy that comes only from religious fervour. As he is a retired senior officer from within the Fire Services, he must have a point.

And so I pose a question. With arrival on our shores of many representatives of the world's faiths, in what is a largely secular society, how are we all to live peaceably together on our small and crowded island? Why, in all humility, cannot mankind derive inspiration from the Prophets[19] draw comfort not contention from the sacred word, and agree on the Laws of Noah[20]?

The question starts in our schools. Emma Kirk, the music teacher in the play is simply happy in her faith. Why can't everyone else be happy in theirs? Can she talk about it in the classroom?

As one teacher put it to me when I asked her how she dealt with the very many faiths that are represented in her school in Leeds, she said "We celebrate everything". Many other teachers probably do the same. That must be much better than not celebrating anything, and much more likely to lead to social cohesion. And, why not some healthy scepticism too? All of this should not worry those who have true faith or real doubt. Sometimes political correctness may just occasionally not be correct.

A number of years ago I heard the following proposition which I endorse here. If there is one God, it shouldn't be outrageous to suggest that for the billions of people on this planet there are many paths to him or to her, just different routes up the same mountain, and that each one is equally valid and each one blessed. The Matterhorn above Zermatt in Switzerland looks quite unlike Monte Cervino in Italy, but it is the same mountain.

The strength of individual belief underpins the validity of one - it does *not* undermine the validity of another. It also underpins its integrity. No single way is exclusive, although Judaism, Christianity and Islam all find words to suggest that theirs is. If they have that belief, isn't it time for them to shed it? A compassionate God – or Allah the All-Merciful - in his wisdom must be allowed some continuing discretion as to whom he admits into his divine presence - now mustn't he?

I cannot believe that God has favourites among his children. There has been and still is too much suffering caused by those who have believed this. We are dealing here with the Infinite. There is no edge to the universe. The concept of God should reflect that. I am happy to echo here sentiments that others, much more learned than me, have expressed, most recently Chief Rabbi Sir Jonathan Sacks in his book, *The Dignity of Difference*[21]

God is not One but, if *n* stands for infinity, One to the power of *n*. That is a thought to unite all those who believe in a supreme deity. In the name of humanity they should rejoice in sharing it. The Alexandria Declaration[22] of the three Faiths was a real start. It needs to continue.

Monotheism stems from tribes in the desert that couldn't live in harmony then any more than they would appear to be able to do so today. The Holy Land is an unholy mess. Jerusalem is not a city of peace. But those tribes produced Holy texts, the Torah, the Bible and the Koran. Beautiful documents. There is an exhibition of them in the British Library as I write. Incredible wisdom in their day, but they contain militant passages right for their day, but out of synch in our global world. They were written when the sun went round the earth, not the other way round, and when bullocks and goats were sacrificed upon an altar. They predate Copernicus, never mind the Hubble telescope and all the scientific discoveries of our times. Furthermore there are some things we are not given to know for sure or at all, and so many things scientists do not know even now[23].

So give Holy texts the respect they deserve, but not now an unquestioning literal obedience if that denies to God's presence compassion, and if it denies to people of other faiths or no faith at all their common humanity. We will need all the help Holy texts can give us if we are to contain HIV Aids and confront the effects of climate change on our psyche, never mind on our landscape and on our financial resources.

So I say where I stand. We should see ourselves as partners on Planet Earth, not rivals, as bringing forth the blessing of tranquillity, not the curse of violence, and the gift of sacred beauty, not the ugly face of conflict. How can you educate a multi-ethnic society in any other way? People should not just come together in prayer only when they mourn their dead in war.

If writing this seems all a bit naïve, I still have a basic conviction in the worth of liberal values. That has nothing whatsoever to do with party politics. These values can be found sometimes, but sadly not always in most political parties. I hope that I am not too naïve asserting them here.

"Care, and take care" is the underlying message within the play. I am not sure that everyone does. Far too many people don't.

If not now, when?

We do need to take very great care of our heritage. Older civilisations than ours, from the East and from the West, respected their ancestors and the earth they came from. We should do the same. We need to reassert some of our own core values, and resurrect some time-hallowed norms. It is not critical whether they are based upon religious precept or simply upon rational judgment. And they are as much about our legacy to the generations to come, as to things we seek for ourselves, often in our own selfish interest.

How many natural or human disasters must take place, how many temples have to be destroyed, before we start to do this? See the final moments of the play in this context.

I toss this tiny pebble into a very large pond. I hope it may cause just a few ripples before it sinks to the bottom.

To close, a little story. Two seriously ill patients go to see a doctor. He examines the first. "Oh dear" he says, "I am most terribly sorry. I *cannot* do anything here." He then sees the second. "Oh dear, oh dear, oh dear. I *must* do something here." Hence a play within a book. Please read it with that in mind. See the whole as one picture, but see it as a fragment of a very large canvas.

Death of a Nightingale

A Play written to be read

Author's note

Why "*A play written to be read*""? This might seem a contradiction in terms. But I am a writer with the writer's wish to write words that will leave the confines of my own four walls, and have a life of their own in the public domain, a bit like an artist's painting. This seems to the best way to achieve that. Also my friends, to whom I am indebted for their comment and criticism, have suffered my obsession for far too long. I retired at sixty hoping to enjoy a quiet life, I am still hoping to do this, and I need to move on for their sake as well as for mine. Consistently with that all royalties will be donated in perpetuity to *Death of a Nightingale Fund*[24] within the *Community Foundation serving Tyne & Wear* to benefit children with special educational needs.

Meanwhile you will have to use your imagination. There will be no stage set or actors to help you.

The world, however, is *your* world, and you have a big advantage over the theatre-goer - you can freeze frame. You can stop the action any time you like, to think about the things you read about. I hope that you will.

Background to the Play

Brighouse School is a small, modern, school for physically disabled children with a learning disability. It has just over 100 pupils and is all-age. Among its facilities is a hydrotherapy pool, a treatment suite that accommodates a school nurse, physiotherapists and speech and language therapists when available. The Office for Standards in Education, OFSTED, has repeatedly sung its praises, especially its ethos. It offers the National

Curriculum and it actively espouses music, the arts and involvement in the community. But it is out of synch with contemporary political thinking about special needs.

The School is the hero of the play. Parents adore it. Other special schools are however just a little jealous of its success. And the Local Education Authority, the LEA, implementing a national policy to reduce the number of children in special schools and then reduce the number of special schools overall, sees it as a natural target. The pupils would be better placed in mainstream schools, or so they think. All of this may be easier to understand if SEN was called Special *very different* Needs.

Brighouse School caters for children who have physical disabilities and learning difficulties associated with them. There are very many of these disabilities. They include cerebral palsy, spina bifida with hydrocephalus, cystic fibrosis, muscular dystrophy, rheumatoid arthritis, heart conditions, osteoagenesis imperfecta, Crohn's disease, epilepsy and neurological disorders. There are also victims of road traffic and other accidents. This is the world of burns and fractures. There are sub-divisions of each disability.

But there are also many other quite different needs and other special schools cater for them, some with a national name and a national reputation. There are children with profound and multiple learning difficulties PMLD, emotional and behavioural difficulties EBD, with hearing problems, speech or sight impairment, sometimes total. There is also dyslexia, dyspraxia and autism. In other words, think of a fruit shop. There are apples, pears, peaches, grapes, bananas and so on. With apples alone, there are coxes, bramleys, and golden delicious et cetera. It's the same thing with SEN.

There are about 400,000 children with learning difficulties of one sort or another. The Department of Health White Paper *Valuing People* envisages an annual increase of around one per cent of children with severe learning difficulties. If their parents want them to be educated in a Special School, they need to receive a Statement.

Statementing is a bureaucratic process under the control of Local Education Authorities (LEAs). It could be, and it should be a multi-disciplinary one, but it isn't. It is regulated by Law and it is designed to define the very different needs of children requiring special attention, and the way those needs are to be met. It is a passport to admission to a special school, that is impossible without it.

A DfES publication *Removing Barriers to Achievement - The Government's Strategy for SEN* reported in the pupil level census in 2003 that there were nearly 94,000 children attending special schools.

For their part, Judges have ruled that children with special educational needs must receive education appropriate to those needs. All of this gives them legal protection and their legal rights - if they can exercise them.

About 100 Special Schools have been closed since 1997. Parental choice? Legal rights?[25] Tell that to the fairies.

CAST

Head teacher and School Governor

Margaret Williamson is 45 years of age. She has experience, charisma, and all the qualifications to be a head teacher. She has a close and intimate relationship with the English teacher, Joan Errington. By and large this is out of school, but known within the school and accepted. She is committed to the School and knows its strengths "The one thing that we can give to our kids is time." She also knows the way the wind is blowing, and she is mindful of her own future career. She suffers from bouts of depression and migraines, but these are managed with medication.

Retired headteacher

Don Smithson - retired head teacher - works for LEA during his retirement. He is in his sixties and he has a warm and friendly style. He is loyal to the system. He still cycles to work with a rucksack, keeping himself fit and active. He used to play cricket for the local club. He is a team man.

Music Teacher

Emma Kirk - black Caribbean extraction. She is charismatic, lively and full of fun.

"You can keep your national curriculum. Just give me music. It's for life and for living." "This country's far too cold, damp, grey and drab. Those banana boats from Jamaica didn't just bring bananas. It's colour, rhythm, vibrancy. It's fun. It's the Notting Hill Carnival. [26]" She is very big, and very huggable. Her laugh can be her cry.

21

English Teacher and School Governor

Joan Errington - 30 years of age, very committed to her job and to the School. She takes a personal interest in some of the pupils and takes them to local theatres. She sees her work as a vocation. She loves and respects the head teacher .She prefers to appear studious with spectacles, rather than attractive with contact lenses.

Non Teaching Care Assistant and School Governor

Wendy Robinson - warm and friendly middle aged woman. She is a salt of the earth type. Her job is to help those children who need toileting and help with eating. She has been involved with children with special needs for many years and loves it. She feels that kids talk to her more than to their teachers and to their parents, and she is probably right.

Pupils

Terry

A pupil with Crohn's disease, age 15. He has truanted from schools he didn't like and which didn't meet his needs. He does not appear disabled. He has lost over one year's education trying to get into Brighouse School.

Johnny

A pupil with *liberator* voice box, age 15. He runs the school newspaper. He has been bullied in mainstream school with jokes about his mechanical voice. He has also been locked in a school cupboard.

Philippa

A pupil in wheel chair, age 15. She has competed in the Para Olympics and won a Silver Medal. She has also competed in Great North Runs, and plays in the School Band.

Tracy

A pupil with cerebral palsy, age 15. She is very bright and has been at the School since she was four.

Harry

A pupil with brittle bones, age 12. He arrives with arm in plaster. He has slipped in the corridor of a mainstream comprehensive school in rush and tumble. He, too, has been bullied. He has been tripped on the stairs which caused him to break his leg, but no-one could prove anything, and the bully got away with it. Parents kept him away from school for his safety.

Parents

Parent Governor

Anwar Fawzi, a Sikh and father of Harry. His wife is Caucasian. He is a taxi driver. He is very worldly, with a keen sense of right and wrong.

Parent

Judith Fawzi, Anwar's wife. She is a nurse at the local hospital She is concerned about her son's repeated fractures. "People should remember that the very first thing a mum asks when her child is born is whether it is OK."

Parent Governor

Gillian (Jilly) James - housewife - mother of Terry. She has a short fuse and she had a fight to get Terry into the School. "I told them that they could look after Terry for me for a week. Then they would know what I have to live with." Her husband is an engineer, often working away from home, leaving her to look after things in his absence.

Other Governors

Chair of Governors

Eileen Winterton is middle aged and a retired law lecturer. She is also a magistrate. She has in her time supported Greenpeace, Anti apartheid, and CND, but she is now not quite such a firebrand. But she has a great sense of right and wrong.

Chair of Finance

Frank Jones owns a small firm of printers and he is very trusting of people. He is a Rotarian. He has a nephew with profound and multiple learning difficulties. He feels that society must look after those most vulnerable. He has two sons going out into the world. He is Yorkshire born and a firm believer in value for money and personal integrity. He always wears a suit with a Rotary badge in his lapel.

Retired NHS Hospital manager

John Lavers is a professional's professional. He does what circumstances demand.

He is very pragmatic and he knows that NHS has a major problem dealing with finite financial and human resources. He sees need for professionals to stick together and help each other. He is always smartly dressed, and sports a regimental tie.

Local and Central Government

National official from DfES

James Harrington is a mandarin, he exudes quiet authority, and he smiles through cold teeth. He was educated at Balliol College, Oxford. His father was a district commissioner in the Punjab during the Raj. He watches his own back very carefully, as well as the backs of others. His job is to deliver policy as quickly as possible. Nothing happens otherwise. Hence *ends justify means* sort of person. His suit, shirt and tie, Savile Row[27]. You would not expect to see him on the Clapham Omnibus[28]. Not the ordinary man in the street.

Regional Official

Judy Fotheringham - age 46 - is very purposeful and ambitious. She wants to deliver official policy. She focuses on outcomes not needs. She is somewhat irritated by those who get in her way. She has a teenage daughter, Rebecca, who she is putting through university. She is a single parent. Her husband died of prostate cancer. She is somewhat overweight.

Director of Education

David Harding - over 40 - is knowledgeable, and has reservations about the policy of Inclusion but knows he has to go with the tide and the Party line. He has a conscience, but he keeps it under strict control. He is a kind man that you can't help liking and respecting, even if he is doing things you don't approve of.

Special Needs Coordinator

Gerry Thompson is young, ambitious, and idealistic, but a little naïve. He will do what he is told. He is quite amoral when it comes to methodology

Clerk to the Governors

Tommy Jeffers is soon to retire. He is a professional, and everyone's friend. He keeps the rule book, and tries to keep to it as best he can. As an officer of the Council, he sees his job as keeping the LEA and governing bodies on the same track, moving in the same general direction.

The settings should be minimalist with the focus on different shapes and sizes of desks and table set against changing window backdrops.

Music before the play begins – "Jamaica Farewell", "Oh Island in the Sun" and "You are my sunshine my only sunshine… " played by steel drum band.

ACT ONE

Scene I

Music room – a new pupil arrives

The Music Room of Brighouse School is set out with guitars and other instruments around the wall. There is also a TV, CD/DVD and speakers.

5 pupils are practising on steel drums for a local gig. Emma Kirk is sitting at an upright piano, shows them calypso rhythm.

EMMA *You know whenever I hear this calypso I hear the sweet voice of Harry Belafonte singing it on his imaginary island in my homeland, in the Caribbean.*

JOHNNY (with liberator) *Isn't this your homeland now?*

EMMA *This is my homeland too. You can have two passports. You can have two homelands. Me is twice blessed. Actually me is three times blessed. God is also my homeland. I am just so sorry for those poor folk who don't have any at all..*

TRACY *Do you still think about the country where your family came from?*

27

EMMA *Sure I do. And I know what my folk must have felt when they came here.*

JOHNNY *What?*

EMMA *Wow, this country's wet and grey. Jamaica, oh fo' Jamaica, where the sun shines all day... and folk sing and dance all night long. Just what sort of a place has this banana boat brought us to?*

TRACY *Well, why did your family come here then?*

EMMA *'Cos people stopped buying our sugar cane. Wasn't worth their while with sugar beet being made cheap here. Still like our rum tho'. That's where our rhythm comes from. Our rum. Come on let's have some rhythm in our music this morning. Imagine you're Trinidadians beating it out on their oil drums.*

They start playing "Island in the Sun".
Headteacher enters with a couple of parents Mr. and Mrs. Fawzi and Harry. Harry is being admitted to the School the following term. He has his arm in plaster.

MARGARET *Sorry to interrupt the fun. This is Mr. & Mrs. Fawzi and Harry. Harry's joining us next term. This is where you can hear our sound of music. Harry's had real bad luck. You have only to look at his bones and they break. He had just mended his leg - broke it when a bully tripped him up on the stairs - and now he's broken his arm, just moving from one lesson to another with a crowd of kids, and he slipped on some chewing gum. He's an accident waiting to happen. Kids tease him like mad. Say he's always "plastered."*

EMMA *He won't get teased here.Not so long as he lets us all autograph his plaster.*

JUDITH *Will Harry be able to join the band?*

EMMA *Not if he's got that plaster on. You know our Band won a Cup in the National Schools Band Competition. With a bit of luck he'll be able to join us when we defend our title next year.*

MARGARET *Can I introduce you to our Tim Pan Ali Band?* (Short beat on the drums by everyone.) *Give our guests a sample of your playing.*

Band plays for a couple of minutes.

This is Tracy. She knows more about the school than I do. Been here since she was four. You know there's a popular view that kids with special needs get on fine in primary schools but the difficulties may come later when they face a different world in the comp. But we are a real alternative even at the primary stage. We've got a highly skilled team here - carers as well as teachers. They put in the groundwork. It bears fruit in later years. Look at Tracy's progress, and you'll see what I mean. She is doing really well.

EMMA *That's very true. The older kids benefit as well for the same reason, and then they all go into the outside world. That's where Inclusion really matters, isn't it? And another thing. Those young kids are helped all along the way, seeing what the older ones can do, being encouraged by them. Saying things we can't.*

MARGARET *You see it happening in the playground, or when they help wheel each other around.*

ANWAR *You're dead right. I've seen it on the school run.*

MARGARET *My philosophy is that there's nothing our kids can't do that mainstream kids can. We had some out abseiling just last week.*

EMMA *They can see for themselves just what's possible with their lives, not what seems impossible. They see our kids leaving this school, getting jobs or going to university. This really gets the young ones trying to do just the self same thing.*

MARGARET *This School is certainly no dead end and there's precious little bullying either. That's a huge blessing.*

EMMA *Some people have described it as a ghetto.*

MARGARET *A ghetto - those people don't know what a ghetto is - and they don't know this School. We're a great big family. That's what we are. A great big happy family. I must tell you about Tracy's great claim to fame. At one of our Presentation evenings - you know we have lots of fun and entertainment as well as prize giving on these great occasions - well, she caught my predecessor full in the face with a custard pie... she was supposed to miss.*

TRACY *He was supposed to duck. I paid the price the following year. I was asked to be Jack in the Box. I was inside that box for ages. He said he forgot I was there. Do you believe that?*

MARGARET *Do you believe anything in this world Tracy? That's one of the lessons we teach you.*

JOHNNY (voice from liberator) *I was locked in a cupboard in my old school. Some classmates they were. The cleaners let me out. It was awful. They called me old crackers box.*

MARGARET *Johnny had a hard time. His mum took him away from school. It was so bad. Finally came here. You wouldn't believe it. He wants to be a journalist. He runs the school newspaper, and the local paper has had him in the newsroom. In this school we believe that kids are capable of anything.*

ANWAR *I can believe that. Have you heard of Fred Raffle? He's a blind man who plays cricket with dried peas inside the ball so you can hear it, and a suitcase as the wicket. He learnt the game at a school for the blind. And my goodness, he now commentates on international cricket. You know, I heard him commentate when India played England. There's guts for you.*

MARGARET *Fantastic. That's exactly what we find here, and what we encourage. I hope mainstream schools find the time to do the same. The trouble is I don't think they always do, and certainly their staff are not always trained to stretch kids. But that's by the way. Here's our athletic hero, Philippa. Tell Mr. and Mrs. Fawzi what you did last year.*

PHILIPPA *Competed in the Athens ParaOlympics, the wheelchair 800 metres.*

TRACY *And won a Silver medal.*

PHILIPPA *Gordon won a Gold in the 4 x 400 relay.*

MARGARET *We had a team of three out there. Gordon Davis did fantastically well. Last but not least there Terry here. He lost one year's schooling while his mum and dad tried to get him in here. Tell the Fawzis about it, Terry.*

TERRY *I've got Crohn's. It's not very nice, but the physio's help here whenever I need it. It's great. The stupid local authority said there was nothing wrong with me.*

MARGARET *Don't say stupid, Terry. But it is what happens when an official of the Council decides these things. There really should be a multi-disciplinary team making these decisions. The Council doesn't want the medical people in on the actual decision taking at all. They actually don't want them to say anything at all to parents. They think it'll cost them money.*

JUDY *Well you know I am a nurse. Nurses are not allowed to suggest a suitable school to parents. Would you believe that?*

MARGARET *I would. Health and Education are two separate worlds. We've got NHS people here, but they are, and they aren't, part of our team.*

JUDITH *Yes and those local authority officials don't really know anything about either of these worlds, if you ask me. They should remember that the very first thing a parent asks when their child is born is whether it's okay. They should remember that.*

ANWAR *They should remember a lot of things. By the way, do they still want to close this School down?*

EMMA *Look guys, I'm sorry but I have got my class to teach. Can you talk about that somewhere else?*

ANWAR *Oh dear, we've interrupted you. But I've enjoyed meeting you and the kids too.*

MARGARET *(Leading the Fawzis out of the door) We'd better leave you to make some more of your music. (Outside the classroom)*

You were asking whether the LEA wanted to close the School. They certainly did, until our parents persuaded them otherwise. It was some campaign. They didn't know what hit them.

JUDITH I read all about it in the local papers.

MARGARET Well, they had been warned. They held a meeting at the school and tried to sell the idea of Inclusion. The parents asked for a vote at the end of the meeting, and all the parents, every single one of them, put up their hands saying that they didn't agree. But, of course, they just went ahead. The parents went mad. They put in a joint letter. The LEA said it never arrived. Can you believe it? Then they went to the great British public, the ones here who know how good this school is, and they got well over 10,000 of them to put in written objections to the school being closed.

ANWAR So how does it stand now?

MARGARET The Minister threw out the closure plan. He pretty well had to. Apart from the public protest, the leaders of the medical profession also opposed it. GPs and the Consultants looking after kids in this school. They knew you see. The GPs had their patients here, and the consultants actually came to the School when they wanted to see their patients.

JUDITH Wow. That's really something.

MARGARET It worked well. When the Consultants visited their patients everyone could come together here, you know, teachers, carers and the School nurse and the physio if they were involved, and the child didn't lose any school time.

JUDITH Wow.

MARGARET Anyway, we still don't know whether all good things will come to an end or whether they won't. All I know is that every day we stay open is a victory for these kids. And if they close this school it will break my heart.

Scene 2

Regional office, DfES – managing Inclusion

There is a desk and a round table and 4 chairs. On the desk there is a photograph of Rebecca, Judy Fotheringham's daughter. Regional officer Judy Fotheringham is first joined by a civil servant from London, James Harrington and then by Director of Education, David Harding, and head of Special Needs Gerry Thompson from Westborough City Council.

After introductions and pleasantries, they discuss the closure of Brighouse School. It has been thwarted by strong campaign by parents to keep it open. Over 15,000 reasoned objections persuaded the Minister to reject plan to close the school.

JUDY (on the telephone) *Yes, I did listen to the repeat of "Yes Minister". I do admire Sir Humphrey.*

James Harrington knocks and enters

JAMES *Are you talking about me?*

JUDY (still on the 'phone) *God has just walked in. I'lll ring you back later. Bye (To James) Hello, good to see you again.*

JAMES *Nobody's ever said I had a divine presence before. Mind you they thought my father had when he was a District Commissioner in the Punjab. But people do turn to me for the occasional miracle. I don't object to being called Sir Humphrey, but I do have to correct you about Yes Minister. We only like to think we're wise and knowledgeable. I am not sure we always are.*

JUDY *Last night's programme was really cruel. Did you see it?*

JAMES *No, I missed it.*

JUDY *It was all about the Dome[29] and Government waste. Hacker was lamenting the fact that the real problem was not the waste of £800m so much as the public view of it. He said the problem was not so much its viability as its visibility. He said it would have been much better if the project* had been constructed underground connecting directly with the new Jubilee Line. The spend might then have been almost totally invisible. Then he went on to say that Hadrian was not so ill-advised as to say that twelve million people would visit his Wall in the year of its completion, and that that venture was a good deal more ambitious than the Dome.

JAMES *You really mustn't allow yourself to be upset by the media. Whenever this arose my father - wise old bird if ever there was one - always said that the Pharaohs weren't put off their grand design for the Pyramids by carping criticism in the Alexandria Times. I'll tell you something else. Have you heard the Latin tag "Audi alteram partem"?*

JUDY *My Latin's not very good these days. Doesn't it mean something like "You have to listen to both sides of the argument"?*

JAMES *Pity you didn't have a classical education. In the civil service manual, it's translated to mean that "you can drive your car on the wrong side of the road. " Politicians watch our backs and we watch theirs. They provide the first line of defence to attack. They take the blame. They provide the safety valve for the system. Then ultimately, if the civil service gets it very badly wrong, they lose their seats. It works. Mistakes self-correct ... as long as you are prepared to wait long enough.*

(David Harding and Gerry Thompson knock and enter.)

DAVID *I hope we're not interrupting.*

JAMES *No we're just acclimatising our minds to living in a very different world from the great British public. It's just a pity they are not more appreciative of what we are trying to do for them.*

DAVID *Sorry we're a bit late. Can I introduce Gerry Thompson? He heads up our Inclusion team. You've met already haven't you, Judy?*

JUDY *Yes, last autumn.*

JAMES *We haven't had the pleasure. I'm so glad you've come. Can we get down to business straightaway? Time's well ... Time.*

JUDY *Of course.*

(They all settle round James).

JAMES *Thank you Judy for setting up this meeting. The Minister suggested that I see you. He does think that this situation needs to be actively managed. He didn't like having to reject your proposals, David, but he really had no alternative.*

DAVID *I agree. I don't hold it against him.*

JAMES *And we don't hold it against you. But we certainly don't want other parents copying them. Fifteen and half thousand objections giving reasons why the school should not be closed, and two TV celebrities and a former international footballer. We can do without that again. We don't mind petition signatures. There can be millions of them so far as we are concerned. Ultimately we just shred them and recycle the paper. It's a great safety valve for the disgruntled. Objections with reasons - that's another matter. Each one of them is shred resistant.*

DAVID *You're dead right, but our political masters say that we have to consult. They just don't realise how wasteful of time this is when parents take the offer seriously. Not just hours, days and days,nights and fucking nights. That's how long it took three people to go through their written objections. And then we had to respond to them all.*

JAMES *That's one of the things that the Department is worried about. We just don't want it to catch on. This is the second time it's happened. It's getting to be a habit, and one we can do without. We've now taken the Minister out of the firing line here and set up School Organisation Committees[30] to deal with school closures and take the flak.*

DAVID *That was a clever move, a gesture to local democracy but making it much easier for us to deal with.*

JAMES *But we still don't want the idea to catch on.*

JUDY *I did have a word with David about that.*

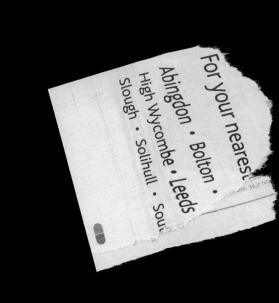

DAVID *Yes and I had a word with the Head. Told her to keep the celebrations local. She got the message that the school should not use the Internet to tell the whole world about it. I told her it would not go down well if they did. She understood.*

JAMES *Good. That's one of the things the Minister was very worried about. The other, of course, is how you get the show back on the road. We need that. You see I was at the UNESCO conference at Salamanca 2 in ninety four. Nearly a hundred countries all saying that children with special needs had a right to mainstream education. That certainly galvanised us into action. I've never seen Parliament move so fast, and so decisively.*

Don't think that the Minister doesn't realise that change can be a bit painful. He knows that in every good parent there is a Luddite[31] trying to get out. In many cases they like what they have but they have no understanding of the world that we are trying to create for them and their kids. It's your job Gerry to illuminate them, to show them the way to truth and light.

GERRY *I know. I had a really good grounding at my university, under Professor Hopwood. A real visionary.*

JAMES *Know him well. He has advised us a number of times.*

DAVID *Yes, we've used him too for training.*

JAMES *Academia has been very supportive. They do know which side of their bread is buttered on. Anyway, the policy of Inclusion could not have a better provenance. Baroness Warnock led the way more than twenty years ago. That's when it was very enlightened. Now there's all party consensus. And it has the full support of all the leading disability organisations. Mind has been particularly helpful. Their President Lord Rix pushed hard for it. He and his daughter had a hard time of it, badly discriminated against by the old system. Blunkett, too.*

GERRY *There's plenty of other parents that feel the same way. Feel their kids should get an equal chance in a mainstream comp.*

DAVID *Of course not all parents agree. That's the basic problem.*

JAMES *People like Gerry will win them over. You just have to. You see the Treasury has made up its mind that there are savings to be made here if they invest in it. You know the figures. Three per cent of children have special needs but they gobble up eight per cent of the total spend on education. That really isn't equitable.*

DAVID *Between these four walls I don't think Inclusion is going to be a cheap option.*

JAMES *Well leading accountants advised us that we could make some real savings simply by reducing the number of Statements LEAs have to write for children with special needs. Get that down by a third, reduce special school places by the same, and then hey presto you don't need all those special schools. And writing Statements is a real headache. We'll have to keep some schools for kids with profound difficulties or very complex behavioural problems, but most can go.*

DAVID *Hm. Accountants. Some are just calculating machines on legs. They play with figures and talk about outcomes. They leave us to deal with people and try to meet their needs. They're just not street wise. They manage us when we should be managing them. The savings won't be there if we do our job. Mark my words.*

JAMES *You may well be right, especially to begin with. The Treasury has agreed to cough up millions to adapt mainstream schools, and we will obviously have to commit ourselves to training. We are currently trying to work out the actual cost now. It's not easy though. There's a major study just started.*

DAVID *Good luck to it. I look forward to seeing the results. I just hope you haven't provided them.*

JAMES *You're a cynic. Anyway, just you keep your doubts to yourself. Money is where money needs to be is my motto. We can't go back now.*

JUDY *And we don't want to.*

JAMES *And that brings us back to Brighouse School and its whingeing parents. What are you going to do?*

JUDY *I thought we could suggest to the Local Council that they bring in a consultant, you know one who would say the right thing, get his recommendations and put them to the School Organisation Committee. Of course, he'd consult first.*

JAMES *I am not sure that that is the best answer. You have got to win over the parents. I think you need something a bit more subtle. Look at it this way. They have a bird in their hands, and they like it. We are offering them, as they see it, two in the bush. Where's their next dinner coming from? Not from the bush unless we make their bird look a bit less appetising.*

DAVID *I hope you are not going to get me into trouble with the Royal Society for the Protection of Birds.*

JAMES *And I hope you are not a covert animal rights activist.*

DAVID *Well what are you actually proposing.*

JAMES *I am not proposing anything.*

DAVID *Suggesting, then.*

JAMES *I'm not suggesting anything either. This is a journey of exploration.*

DAVID *Or a safari where the wild beasts roam.*

JAMES *And vultures fly overhead ready to scavenge their next meal. Come on, it's up to you how you manage this. Basically if a lot of the kids in this school go to mainstream schools this school is just not going to be viable. You know that. It can't be making best use of your financial resources. You are just going to have to push things along a bit faster in that direction. It'll be unpleasant, but really run the School down. When you finally deliver the message that the School has to close there'll be no great argument.*

DAVID *It'll actually run itself down, as we admit fewer kids to it. Some redundancies will be unavoidable and they won't be able to deliver the national curriculum.*

GERRY *The bird's already beginning to look a bit sick. Their roll came down last year by nine pupils.*

JAMES *The key is to get the Headteacher on side. You really must try to do that.*

DAVID *To get the egg to accept the frying pan. You're right. The parents have got a lot of time for her. They trust her. If she argues the case for closure it will be much, much better than if we do. And the staff will go along with it too. There should be no problem getting the School Organisation Committee[14] to go along with the closure after that.*

JAMES *She must know that virtue has its reward but definitely not otherwise. She will need another school when the School is closed. You do write her references, after all.*

DAVID *Yes, we do. But that's a trade secret. Governors might do it more knowledgeably, maybe more honestly. We do it more ...er purposefully.*

JUDY *I understand that her nick name is Queen Margaret?*

DAVID *So rumour has it.*

JAMES *Do you mean gossip?*

DAVID *I mean it's on the grapevine. It's what her colleagues call her - not to her face, of course. We didn't know that when she got the job. I don't think there's a problem here.*

JAMES *But it's useful. Look, I don't want to be involved in the fine details of all this. But do keep me informed and we'll watch your backs for you. OFSTED won't cause you any trouble. Oh, one other thing, do try and marginalise the governors. They won't like what you are doing..*

DAVID *By then it will be too late.*

JUDY *Can we all meet again to progress this?*

JAMES *It's really up to the LEA but I don't mind keeping an eye on things. I will certainly do what I can to help behind the scenes if you need me to. I don't think we need a minute of this meeting.*

DAVID *Could you drop me a note just confirming that it has taken place?*

JAMES *I'll send you something suitable, a comfort letter if that is what you'd like. It won't be very explicit.*

DAVID *That's okay.*

JAMES *You are a cautious bastard.*

DAVID *Bastard today, war wounded tomorrow unless I am careful.*

JAMES *Come on, cheer up. All's fair in love and politics.*

DAVID *Where's the love?*

JAMES *Look, you are more than half way up the pecking order. You should be enjoying life.*

DAVID *You're near the top. You're one of the really lucky ones.*

JAMES *I've still got a few old scars, it's true. Not many people peck at me these days and of course my job is to see they don't peck the Minister either. It's called the art of self preservation. Anyway nothing specific in writing please, and definitely no emails. Oh, by the way, the Treasury has agreed to cough up some more grant aid for those authorities able to progress Inclusion.*

DAVID *I had already heard that.*

JAMES *We do everything we can to help. I must be off. There's a train at noon. Can you get me to the Station? A very good use of time today. Thanks again for everything ... and good luck.*

JUDY *Ask Susan next door. She'll book a taxi for you.*

JAMES *Will do. Thanks.*

(James Harrington leaves the Room)

DAVID (with a smile) *You know, James Harrington is totally, totally without shame.*

JUDY *I don't agree. He's probably a bit like me. I'm not immune to shame. Very, very occasionally I do take my conscience to bed with me, but when I do, and it isn't very often, I leave it on the breakfast table the following morning. We're always going to be upsetting somebody, not meeting their needs. It's in the nature of our job. We're interested in outcomes. Fortunately for us, most of those people who don't like what we're doing just sound off in the pub. Our life would be impossible if everyone was like the parents in your school.*

GERRY *I'm absolutely certain his visit won't give him any sleepless nights at all. Most likely he'll go back home, and open a bottle of Chateau Mouton Rothschild.*

DAVID *Well, Merlot Chateau Sainsbury for me. I'm sure you're right.*

GERRY *We couldn't do without people like Harrington. Nothing would get done. I'm sure that fella will go places.*

DAVID *In this world or the next? You know I believe his father was high up in the Indian Civil Service. That's where he must have got his superiority complex. Tell me; is that a photo of your daughter?*

JUDY *Yes, Rebecca. Putting her through university.*

DAVID *What's she studying?*

JUDY *Bio-engineering. A chip off the other old block. Her father was a lecturer in chemistry. He passed away, last year. Prostate cancer. Took him early. He didn't have a PSA test until too late.*

DAVID *I'm sorry. I didn't know. It must have been difficult.*

JUDY *It was, but the job helped, and it's so much more important to me now. Of course I've got Rebecca. She's been wonderful, but she's left the nest*

DAVID *Bio engineering must be better than social engineering.*

JUDY *A bit more ambitious. Helping the Planet and all that..*

GERRY *Good on her.*

JUDY *Anyway, we've still got to deal with our little patch of it.*

DAVID *You're right. We've got a little engineering of our own to do, haven't we? I don't think that there's anything more to discuss at this time.*

JUDY *No, it's over to you now.*

DAVID *Gerry?*

GERRY *No, I think that's everything.*

DAVID *My Chair is coming in this afternoon. We need to get on the road.*

(David rises from his chair)

JUDY *I don't think that what we have been talking about is what he needs to know.*

DAVID *I'll tell him of our good close working relationship. He'll be pleased.*

(David Harding and Gerry Thompson leave to go.)

JUDY *And let's keep it that way. Keep in touch. By the way, there's a speed trap on North Road just past the Golden Lion. You need to watch for it..*

DAVID *Thanks for that. I do try to be a law abiding citizen. Bye*

GERRY Bye.

(Exit David and Gerry)

JUDY *Better them than me.*

Scene 3

Staff Room – a mood of unease

There are comfortable chairs around the room. A coffee machine is in one corner. It is shortly after 4pm. Joan Errington, Emma Kirk and Wendy Robinson are relaxing.

WENDY *You're the teachers. How do you explain to a ten year old what nanotechnology is?*

JOAN *Revisit Gulliver's Travels or visit Google. Then get him to explain it to you.*

EMMA *Compare it to "no-see-ums" when you're sunbathing on the beach in Jamaica, and they dance the Conga where you least want them. Who wanted to know?*

WENDY *John Turnbull, the boy who controls his wheelchair and his computer with a wand attached to his forehead. He is just so bright. His mum was really chuffed to see his progress when she came in yesterday. My little flower was such a happy little boy.*

JOAN *He has such a lovely smile. The one thing we can give kids like John is time, and that's the reward. Anyway, coffee girls.*

(Nods all round as Joan pours out coffee.)

(Head teacher comes storming in.)

MARGARET *One for me too, Joan dear … and strong. I need it. Thank you for staying behind. It does help to share our thoughts about things now and again. God, that Terry James is impossible. How can you teach a class with him in it?*

EMMA *What's he been up to now?*

MARGARET *I asked him to describe an earthquake. Do you know what he said? "When my dad came home drunk." I then made a big mistake. I asked*

43

him what a volcano was then. And he said "My Mam, when my dad came home drunk".

WENDY *It's not a joke. Have you seen his dad? He must be all of 20 stone.*

MARGARET *Mostly beer*

WENDY *If there's an earthquake in that family it'll be all of seven on the Richter scale. He's great when he is sober. Life and soul of the party. When he's had too many, he is the party.*

MARGARET *And you've seen his mum. When she blows her top, talk of molten lava. But he's still a terrible handful in class.*

WENDY *Isn't he just a naughty kid? I know more about him than you do. When you toilet kids they talk to you, and Terry talks to me more than he talks to you. I mean really talks. You know his home must be bedlam. I don't think his mother can cope.*

MARGARET *Neither can I. He's a bundle of mischief whatever the cause.*
.

EMMA *Same in my book, I'm afraid.. I've got everyone singing DO RE ME and he goes ME RE DO.*

MARGARET *And he shouts. And never sits still for a moment.*

WENDY *Well, I do have to toilet him more than any other kid in the school. I don't know where he gets it all from.*

MARGARET *He's probably a secret beer drinker - he'll take after his father mark my words - Beer's a diuretic you know. Anyway I had a word with nurse about him. She thinks he's a candidate for Ritalin".*

EMMA *There's far too many kids on that these days. It's getting like chewing gum.*

MARGARET *They need to be.*

EMMA *I'm not sure it's not because they haven't got a father.*

MARGARET *Or they've got two.*

JOAN *I hope you two are not getting a bit prissy about single parent families.*

EMMA *You're right. I do like the traditional family. I'm not judging folk when I say that. I'm not preaching. I'm just being practical. I just feel that this would be a far better place if more folk were married. Being married is setting out on a long journey. Why do folk have to get off at the first stop? I remember an old saying from the Ononaga Nation: with every decision you make, keep in mind the Seventh Generation of children to come. I don't think folk think properly about the first generation, never mind the seventh.*

JOAN *No, Emma, maybe you should do more to encourage marriage. That would take guts today, but the breakdown of the family doesn't fully explain Ritalin. The world that kids grow up in today is a very different from the one we grew up in when Ritalin wasn't even around.*

WENDY *Yes, nothing remotely like it.*

JOAN *Every generation has its own battles. Our parents had World War II. It wasn't easy for them. Today's kids face an entirely different world, and it's a very difficult one.*

EMMA *They've got no faith to guide them. That's the trouble.*

JOAN *Or to lead them up the garden path.*

EMMA *No sense of awe, Joan. It's a great loss.*

JOAN *That's certainly true. Once upon a time miracles were, well, miraculous. Today they are the latest piece of technological wizardry.*

EMMA *So right. Once you knew how things worked, and what they did for you. I knew how a car engine worked, even a jet engine. Now not worth trying to find out, even though there's jobs out there for them that knows.*

WENDY *Have you a clue how a cell 'phone actually works, Emma? Or a micro-chip? It's bad enough trying to work through a gobbledegook manual.*

You know, one from Sony or AEG in umpteen languages, and not one of them in simple English. They should have a nice easy version for old timers like me.

EMMA *Yes, you know all those books written for Dummies, well they had me, Emma Rose Kirk, personally in their minds when they wrote them.*

JOAN *And nothing seems to last before it's overtaken by some new revolutionary gizmo, and then you've got to learn it all over again.*

EMMA *Too true. I've just bought an IPod for my music.*

JOAN *Certainly jobs don't last. Downsizing, isn't that the word firms use these days before they sack you? It's difficult to know what you are learning for.*

MARGARET *Sorry to interrupt you. This is a good moment. We're supposed to be having a staff meeting tomorrow. I don't think we want to keep chewing the cud about the future of the school, do we? I thought we could make this a little training session instead. Would you like that?*

(Everyone nods in agreement.)

MARGARET *Okay. Can we focus on motivation? We know kids have a lot of anger, a lot of aggression. And not just kids. What do we do with it? Do we harness it, or do we suppress it? Would that be a good topic?*

EMMA *Yes, it would. Can I give you a story to tell them? It will make a good starting point. It comes from a book I've been reading. The story comes out of Africa. "Every morning a gazelle wakes up. It knows that it must run faster than the fastest lion, or it will be killed. Every morning a lion wakes up. It knows that it must run faster than the slowest gazelle or it will starve to death. It doesn't matter whether you are a lion or a gazelle. When the sun comes up, you better start runnin'."*

MARGARET *I'm afraid Emma, that begs the question - just where do you run to?*

EMMA *If you want to talk about motivation, Margaret, talk sport. Most folk will follow that. So where does Tiger Woods run? To the winning post. That* man knows what it is to aspire - it's not about dosh - no way, and not just to be the best golfer on the day. Tiger wants to be the best golfer ever - and a black. Wow. That's where that man channels all his energy, and he has no fear of failure. He's practised the word 'failure' right out of his vocabulary. If you're afraid of failure you'll win nuttin'. The dustbins are full of the hopes of those who in their bellies were dead scared of failing. They couldn't zap their fears. Sisters, I tell you, if you cannot zap those gremlins right out of your system, you'll win nuttin' in life.

JOAN Yes, you're right about using sport. I heard Navratilova explain why so many good tennis players come out of Eastern Europe. And we produce scarcely any. They have belief and determination, and they don't quit. That's where you run.

EMMA I know another part of the trouble. It's them folk that prattle on about the evils of capitalism and competition. Oh yes it is. That's why we don't win things. Why we have so few sporting heroes of our own. If we want to enjoy them, we have to import them. Then call the football team Chelsea. Them folk, the poor little lambs that have lost their way, baa baa baa. They don't like competition. Poor little things. Tell that to the Chinese. Today their students are keeping our universities going. Why? To compete. Competition's a part of life. Wanting to be somebody is part of real living. Earning and spending our dosh makes the world go round, now don't it? Sure these things are not the be all and the end all, but those folk who moan on about these things are just running scared of life They expect the State to tie their bootlaces for them. That's no good way to be. Now is it?

MARGARET I don't entirely agree. Some people like life without the spills and they don't mind missing out on the thrills. They don't think life should be about winners and losers.

EMMA Okay, but don't wish it on other folk. That is one of the things that life is about. If they don't believe it is, and they're teachers, they're preparing kids for a world that don't exist. You need a horizon. The sting of failure is a spur to glory. Sure you feel the sting, but you're not running scared of it. If you don't like the sting at all, well don't look for the glory. Hey, that's one reason why we celebrate so many victories in this school, isn't it so? We compete. Our Para Olympian medallists for a start. Our Band....

JOAN *You're right There's real triumph when it comes out of adversity, especially if you have to suffer a little first It sets kids up for life. Mollycoddle them, wrap them up in cotton wool, and everyone else will run off with the medals. I think it was Helen Keller³³ who said "Security is an illusion. Life is either a daring adventure or it is nothing at all." She rose to a challenge didn't she? Blind and deaf from early childhood.*

EMMA *Nannies should stay in the nursery, if you ask me. It ain't no good pretending that life's easy. The easy option is usually a dead end. For our kids it is.*

MARGARET *Well there are certainly no cheers for mediocrity. Great Britain wasn't great just because of her Empire and the Maxim gun. Can I sum this up? Unless you find a mountain to climb, you'll never ever find out what you're really capable of. You'll miss out on an awful lot For our kids those mountains are just a little bit higher, and we have to keep reminding them about the view from the top.*

JOAN *Before we finish, Margaret, there's one other thing we should talk about. It you're thinking about motivation, you should also think about things that demotivate. You know the worst thing? And at Brighouse we can see this more clearly than most. It's envy. Envy gets you nowhere, nowhere at all. Margaret, when you opened this discussion you mentioned anger and aggression. Envy sometimes turns that right in on itself. Think of Iago in Othello. The Bard saw it all.*

EMMA *The Bible got there long before that. The Tenth Commandment. Thou shalt not covet. No sin in owning Just sin in coveting.*

MARGARET *No sin in owning? How do you get your camel through the eye of a needle, Emma?*

EMMA *Those gates of Heaven are still a titchy bit open for those rolling in it. It's not owning riches that's the problem. It's what you do with them. Money makes the world go round. I'll tell you something. I know the Bible says you can't serve God and Mammon. It doesn't say it's a sin to go shopping with it. Anyway, that's not the point I'm making. You've got to admire what folk make of their lives when they make a success of it.*

JOAN *Well our kids go along with that. It's so much healthier to rejoice in someone else's achievement than to envy it. And they do, they really do. And we have to encourage it all the time.*

MARGARET *Yes we do. It's liberating for all of us. It's our gift to the world to help people to see that. There is far too much envy about these days - and it's usually the same lost sheep you were talking about. You'd think it was a crime to want to win something. And you'd think it was a sin to want to own a yacht. The great thing these days is that lots of people do, and not just millionaires. It what gets them going. Fly a plane, cure a sick animal, drive a McLaren, just have a dream. That's why you'll want to learn. The tragedy today is that not enough kids have a dream*

WENDY *A lot of our kids do. The young ones get them from the older ones. Good on them all. Any road, I got my dream. We love our van. We have smashing times.*

MARGARET *Exactly. Meanwhile our great government can't make up its mind whether we are a part of one large sausage machine, or a lot of small sausage machines, and they keep coming up with more and more paper plans, more and more targets.*

WENDY *They certainly keep themselves fully employed. Good intentions maybe, but so had my Aunt Mabel.*

MARGARET *Who is your Aunt Mabel, Wendy?*

WENDY *She doesn't actually exist. But in our family we always blamed her when things went wrong.*

MARGARET *No, she exists alright. She works alongside Murphy. Did you not know? I'll tell you exactly where she is. Mum wants little Johnny to come to this school. Thinks it'll meet Johnny's needs. The medics agree. We agree, and we've got a place for him - and the more kids in this school the less on average each one costs. Yes? But no, Murphy who's not wired up to what we do decides the fate of little Johnny and wants to send him somewhere else, and Mabel, who of course is legally qualified, chairs the tribunal that decides what's in Johnny's best interests so long as it makes the best use of economic resources,, and she goes along with Murphy. Mabel's word is final.*

But you can appeal against it. To whom? I'll give you one guess....To the ever courteous, totally dependable Mabel. The needs of little Johnny are supposed to be paramount, but they get lost somewhere along the way. What a crazy mixed up world. They'll give the job to a computer next. You watch.

EMMA *Hey stop this. We're not politicians and sociologists. I just want somebody to let me teach.*

JOAN *That's a real cry from the heart.*

EMMA *I'll bet you most teachers would say the same.*

MARGARET *Sorry girl, you've got to be a sociologist today if you want to be a teacher. You've got to know how people tick, and you've got to know the real world - not the fantasy world you'd like it to be. That's where our kids are going to be and they, especially them, need all the help we can possibly give them..*

JOAN *I wholeheartedly agree, Margaret. You have to be a sociologist, a psychologist, and a fairground manager too.*

WENDY *How about a zoo keeper as well?*

MARGARET *Well Terry James certainly goes into the monkey house so far as I am concerned. And I'd put his mum in with the tigers. I don't know how I keep my cool with her. I keep telling her to try and control her son.*

JOAN *She's not a single mum though.*

MARGARET *No, she's not, but her hubby's away on the rigs an awful lot of the time. And you know what he does with his money when he gets back home. He's the bread winner, but I don't think he contributes much to bringing up their kids. She's got to look after them, and there is four of them.*

JOAN *I feel sorry for her and for her son.*

MARGARET *I feel sorry for me.*

JOAN *For heaven sake, Margaret, relax a little. Share Terry's problems with some of the health professionals. They may have an answer.*

MARGARET *I will. Can we please change the subject?*

EMMA *Look, you three are governors, what's going to happen to our School now the Minister's thrown out the LEA's plans to close it? I need my job. I need a job.*

MARGARET *That's on our agenda for our next meeting.*

EMMA *What do you think is going to happen then?*

WENDY *I've a friend whose husband is a Labour Councillor. She thinks they've still got it in for this school ...even though they say they haven't.*

JOAN *They cannot want another battle with our parents, surely?*

MARGARET *I don't know what they are going to do. I don't think we're in their good books though. We've just got to stick together.*

JOAN *That's not going to be so easy if our numbers keep going down.*

MARGARET *True, but it'll reduce our budget.*

WENDY *And that means redundancies.*

MARGARET *Well - job losses in some form or other. That wouldn't be good for us.*

JOAN *Our parents will want us to make the best of it. I know what they think will happen to our kids if the school closes. They think that some will go to mainstream schools and may be okay, but they know that some won't be. They think that probably all of them will be bullied at some time or another, and that some will go to a different special school that won't be right for them, won't be anything like as good as this one in meeting their needs. That's what they think.*

MARGARET *I'm afraid you're dead right about the bullying. The problem is chronic despite all the efforts to put a stop to it.*

JOAN *Read William Golding's Lord of the Flies to understand. It's the dark side of some kids ...and some grown ups too. I'm afraid it's the beast in them, and it's always going to be there. Putting our kids into mainstream schools simply gives them more kids to bully. That's why the problem, if anything, is getting worse.*

MARGARET *It's not surprising some kids truant, is it? And their mums and dads are taken to court.*

JOAN *And if they don't truant they will have to manage with supply teachers who don't know them, teachers who haven't enough time for them, haven't been fully trained for them, and teaching assistants who don't know how to stretch them.*

MARGARET And *at what cost? They don't come cheap.*

WENDY *And what about training? Will all the staff know how to lift and carry? And what about health? You don't find a school nurse in every school, now do you? I can just see teachers wanting to give valium anally as nurse does here. And of course the physio isn't full time. Will she be there when you want her?*

JOAN *Yes, the great thing here is that our kids can get some stretching exercises between lessons, and when they want them.*

WENDY *Just how much time do physio's waste just travelling from school to school? There's not so many of them. And I'll tell you another thing. There'll be no-one like Mary Turnbull to show them how to bake tarts. No domestic science in the national curriculum. That's the sort of education our kids need – how to manage when you leave school. That's what our kids need, isn't it?*

MARGARET *I share all your fears, I do, I really do, and I am afraid you're right about those that go to another special school. They will end up in schools with PMLD kids, you know the ones with very low IQ, or with emotionally disturbed kids, and it just won't be the right school for them. Oh yes, there'll be some success stories, some great anecdotes, they'll parade* them like Lotto winners, but in today's world no-one will want to talk about the ones that have gone wrong, will they? Now will they? I can't sleep at night through worrying about it. I just can't. Insomnia at night and migraines during the day. Ugh. And pills to keep me company.

JOAN *It's a worry for all of us, Margaret. How on earth can parents plan for their kids' future?*

WENDY *It's a fucking nightmare. And how can we plan for our mortgage repayments?*

JOAN *It's a nightmare, one you never wake up from, however hard you try. So what should the governors do if they still try to close us down?*

MARGARET *I don't think there's anything to be gained ending up on another collision course. No-one would thank us for that and no-one will win. But maybe we can play for time. Every day this school stays open is, as I always say, a victory for the kids who are here now. And we can try to get some more kids admitted, if we can help parents persuade Mabel to let them come. You have to try.*

And I hope the governors will keep telling the LEA the facts of life. What our kids need. What they are entitled to. What their parents can demand. And we can keep the School in the public eye with another Open Day.

JOAN *I agree. I'll back you there.*

WENDY *Me too. No bloody surrender.*

MARGARET *No, the governors mustn't just throw in the towel. That would be awful. If only our lords and masters would listen a bit more. The trouble with civil servants is they are not street wise, clever maybe, but not street-wise. They're cocooned from reality.*

JOAN *They're Cuckoo, you mean.*

MARGARET *No, I wouldn't say that. Many of them are trapped like we are. Trapped by the system.*

JOAN I *think they are led by the wrong people, misled. There's either far too much passion, or far too much reason, but not enough of both together. Did you ever read Khalil Gibran's 'The Prophet'? Do you remember he wrote "Reason alone is a force confining; and passion unattended is a flame that burns to its own destruction."*

MARGARET *Yes, that's a beautiful way of putting it. You know in Education there is actually unreason.*

JOAN *I read an article recently by one of our clever, clever wise guys - far too many of them in education, and too clever by half for our own good, if you ask me. He said - children with special needs come in tens, scores, even hundreds, not one by one. He said you've got to give up the individualised approach. Would you believe it?*

MARGARET *Yes, I know. And I am afraid that some academics just don't understand, and of course they go on to teach their students the error of their ways No doubt they then get their students to repeat those errors to pass their exams. Ugh.*

JOAN *Yes, well I wrote a letter to the paper saying that he should teach kids in special schools like ours not teach about them. You know what he also said? He said the government needed a robust policy to deal with them. A "robust" policy for kids like ours, that was his word. People use the word "robust" today when they should say "ruthless."*

MARGARET *And heartless.*

JOAN *It's Wizard of Oz stuff. You know, the man without a heart and the man without a brain.*

MARGARET *And the Wizard's lost his wand.*

JOAN *That's not the only thing he's lost.*

WENDY *And no yellow brick road for our kids. More to the point, as you said Margaret, the interest of our kids are supposed to be paramount? They've forgot that.*

EMMA Oh *come on, let's stop moaning. Moaning Minnies the lot of us. Anyway time waits for no woman. I've some lessons to mark. I must be off - singing " We'll meet again, don't know where, don't know when, but I know we'll meet again some sunny day."*

MARGARET *So must I.*

MARGARET and EMMA (singing) *"Somewhere over the rainbow - way up high - there's a land that I heard of once in a lullaby Somewhere over the rainbow skies are blue. And the dreams that you dare to dream - really do come true Some day I'll wish upon a star - and wake up where the clouds are far behind me. Where troubles melt like lemondrops - away above the chimney tops - that's where you'll find me."*

Scene 4

Music Room - a music lesson

Emma Kirk is sitting in front of Terry, Johnny, Philippa and Tracy.
Lesson illustrated by CD and DVD recordings

EMMA *Our last lesson was all about mood and atmosphere created by music or captured in music. Can you remember any of it?*

TERRY *I remember Mars God of War from the Planets.*

PHILIPPA *Trust you to remember that one. I remember Sinfonia Antarctica. It gave me the shivers.*

EMMA *Who was it by?*

PHILIPPA *Vaughan Williams.*

EMMA *Good, both of you. I'm really going to open up your ear drums this fine morning. The music I am going to play for you to today will reach parts of you that that well known beer won't reach.*

TERRY *Worth a try Miss.*

PHILIPPA *Oh shut up, Terry*

EMMA *I'm talking about the thing that separates the human race from the animal kingdom. And, even more important, it's where all people can come together. I call it the spiritual side of music. The spirit of God is in this music, or the human spirit. Call it either. In my book they are the same thing. It's the music itself, or it's the people who perform it, like you do. It's the music that some people sing to God. It's also the music they play for each other. It's the music of joy and the music of sadness. You will sense triumph over adversity and yes discord as well as harmony. It's the music that carries the beat of life itself. We are going to start with harmony. You see the great thing about music is that it has no boundaries. It is universal. Listen to* **Music has no boundaries** *sung by* **Ladysmith Black Mambazo**. *Those guys won two Grammies, and performed at two Nobel Peace Prize ceremonies. That piece* of music comes out of South Africa, but If you want to find your God, if there is a God, listen to good music from anywhere in the big wide world.

TERRY *Do you really believe in God, Miss?*

EMMA *Well if she does exist, she wears many different costumes.*

PHILIPPA *I thought God was a "him"*

TRACY *"Hymns is what you sing to God."*

PHILIPPA *A "He" then.*

EMMA *God is whatever you want God to be: He, She or It.*

TERRY *My dad doesn't believe that God exists*

EMMA *She doesn't if you don't believe in her. She does if you do. My folk believed in God and saw God as the Father. For me though God is a mother. I think today you've got to bring religion a wee bitty up to date. After all, Mothers know all about the pain of creation, don't they? The Bible's a great book. But there's far too many men in it. Anyway I'm not sure that 'believe' is the right word. I know she's there. The spirit of God is in every living thing. You just have to listen out for her. But you can turn your back on her too. It's your choice.*

TERRY *I've chosen. (He gives the thumbs down sign)*

EMMA *When you listen to more music you may change your mind. I believe that the hand of God has actually touched the great composers and musicians, and made them great, and for certain not the hand of Charlie Darwin. I heard that great opera singer Placido Domingo say he believed his voice came from God. Music comes up from the earth itself - just listen to this –* **Giving and taking by Tibetan monks of Garden Shartse & Corciolli.** *Those voices come right out of God's good earth, don't they? They remind us, we don't just take from the earth; we have to give back to it. Yes, music comes from deep down in the earth, but it sure reaches right up to those angels in Heaven – now just listen to this. It's not church music but it's often played in church.* **Bach's Toccata and Fugue on the Organ.** *Those* *angels dance in heaven every time that's played in a Cathedral. Can you tell me another heavenly piece of music?*

TERRY *'Ave... a Bloody Mary*

EMMA *Now I'll have no blaspheming in my class. Say "Ave Maria" Terry.*

TERRY *Ave Maria*

EMMA *That's much better. Another one?*

PHILIPPA *I heard Agnus Dei on Classic FM. I think by Faure. It was so lovely.*

EMMA *Very good. I'm sure it must have been the Faure Requiem. There's the joy of the human spirit too - just listen to this.* **Schubert's the Trout.** *And there's tragedy, the Holocaust, you know where millions of Jews, gypsies, and kids just like you were murdered because they didn't belong to the master race. Listen to* **John Williams's Schindler's List.**

TRACY *That's really sad.*

EMMA *Listen to an orchestra. Really listen to it. You won't just hear violins, brass, woodwinds, drums. Every instrument has its own melody. Even the little triangle. That's where the colour comes from. There's harmony and there's discord. Why are people so afraid of discord? In Jamaica I learnt that you needed spice as well as sugar. You know three or four drops of Tabasco in your tomato juice. Discord is part of life and its part of music too. Gives it its drama. Why run away from it. Listen to the* **Rite of Spring by Stravinsky.** *Its first audience tried to run away from it, but they had nowhere to go. Nowhere at all. Would you have booed it or cheered it?*

TRACY *I'd like to have played my drum in it.*

JOHNNY *Me, too. That would have been cool.*

TRACY *You mean hot.*

EMMA *You've got the message. That is why Music is the pulse of life itself. You can hear its beat in classical music and in Jazz and the Blues. You know something - there's plenty of fine music in Heaven and down here on earth, but not one single bar of it in Hell.*

And I'll tell you kids something else you don't appreciate; there's the beauty of music and there's beauty in silence too. The still moment when there is no music, when there is no sound.

TRACY *I don't get that.*

EMMA *I'll tell you what my teacher once said to me. Sometimes a piece of music ends with a big noisy climax. But sometimes it just dies away ever so softly. She said, you'll go to a concert and see this, and you'll hear it. And I have. The conductor holds his baton, the players hold their position, and the audience holds its breath. It's a golden moment. In that God given moment you touch eternity. And that's what I truly felt.   After what seems an eternity, the conductor drops his baton, the orchestra drop their hands and the audience bursts into applause. The moment has gone, but it was there. You'll get the same feeling, the same still moment, when you stand in front of a really great work of art.*

JOHNNY *In front of Tracy Emin's bed?*

EMMA *That bed certainly was not for ever, but you'll feel that some things are, like my island in the Caribbean, like the ebb and flow of the tides lappin' the shore, like the rippling streams that flow into our turbulent oceans, like the rocks and boulders that shape our mountains, like all of nature - its unbelievable beauty, its incredible power,   just its infinite variety - it should leave you with a sense of awe at its majesty. These are for ever God's gifts to you and to me, to all mankind, yes, and without distinction between believer and unbeliever, between rich and poor. And, you guys, they are for ever, for ever. (*Very softly then absolute silence*)

TRACY (Drops drum stick) *Sorry.*

EMMA *Never mind. God's just left the room!*

TERRY *But God's gifts kill.*

EMMA *They also heal. You can't have a world just made out of sugar candy.*

TERRY *It's more like my mam's suet pudding.*

PHILIPPA *Do you pray to God?*

EMMA *Do I pray to her? Well I know that lots of folk don't, and they can tell me I am a nutter, but I talk to Her every day. I say a few words to Her every morning and I say a few more before I go to bed. Just tell Her what I've been gettin' up to. The cares of the day just disappear. Better than taking those goodnight pills I can tell you. And on Sundays I sing Her praises. Just listen to the* **Agnus Dei** *from the* **Faure Requiem.** *You are so right Philippa. I'll tell you something else. I talk to her and She talks to me. She talks to everyone, yes everyone, if they care to listen. Not just to Moses and Jesus and Mohammed. We have quite a chat at times. You give her a call sometime, and you'll see.*

TERRY *My Dad thinks that people who hear voices are bonkers.*

EMMA *He thinks what he thinks. I think what I know.*

TRACY *My Nana used to say that God was as near to her as a new born babe and as far away as the furthest star?*

EMMA *I like your Nana. She was a wise one, that lady. She knew, like I do.*

PHILIPPA *Do you pray for this School?*

EMMA *Sure I do. Every single day I pray for this school, and I pray for you.*

TERRY *My mam said you're leaving us.*

TRACY *No!*

EMMA *Gossip. Some people have nothing better to do than wag their tongues. There's a job going, and I've put in for it. I don't think I'll get it. I've got a life sentence here bringing music to you kids, a life sentence with hard labour. Now what was I saying before I was rudely interrupted? I pray for this School, and I pray for all schools. Music's gone missing from many of them these days.*

TRACY *Maybe they didn't have anyone like you to teach them when they were at school.*

EMMA *Yes that must be it. Seriously the more our political wonder kids assert the national curriculum, targets and league tables, the more music loses out. Now, let's get back to the spiritual side of music, music that's the same the world over, like people are. Folk music, the same rhythms you'll find in every little village wedding over centuries of time. It's not clever to give up on those weddings, you know. Anyway, folk music's now in the soul.*

Now I remember my Daddyo recounting how he heard the great Black American singer Paul Robeson deliver that same message in Peekskill, a little town in New York State, at a big open air concert[32] Now, not everyone likes being told that they are all God's children. There's always some that don't. And on that day those folk came out in force with their clubs, their rocks and their stones, and they rained them down on those peaceful concert goers, on little children too, as they made their way home.

TRACY *No. Why did they do a terrible thing like that?*

EMMA *Well, some people just don't believe in a universal creator. They believe in their own tribal God. That's always making for trouble and suffering. Anyway, that's all half a century ago. I'm sure times have changed in Westchester County. But what Paul Robeson said about folk music fifty years ago is just as true today. Let's get back to it. You see, one of the earliest gifts God gave to mankind was music.*

TERRY *Was it a Christmas present Miss?*

EMMA *Oh for heaven's sake, Terry, it was a gift to Christian, Jew, Muslim, Buddhist, and to non-believer from that day to this; no-one any different. It was a gift then, and it's a gift today to every new born child, even before it's born, when it's still in the womb.*

TRACY *Can they hear it?*

EMMA *Yes they sure can. And when they grow up, they'll sing it, they'll dance to it and maybe they'll play it. Have you heard of the Israeli Violinist Yitzhak Perlman? He plays in concerts all round the world. Do you know something?*

He goes on to every stage he plays on, on crutches. He got polio as a child. Didn't stop him playing. Just listen to this, from Eastern Europe. Some say that its origins go way back to Bible times. It's called **Klezmer – Honga Encore.**

I'd love it if you played a musical instrument. You'd love it. In an ideal world you'd even get free tuition. They say they are concerned about "the have nots." They should call them "the never haves." And never will have, the way things are going.

TERRY *I think people should have a right to learn music at school.*

EMMA *People talk a lot about human rights these days. But you never hear them talk about the right to music. It is as important as any.*

TRACY *What if you are deaf?*

EMMA *Haven't you heard of Evelyn Glennie? She can't hear a thing she plays, not a single note. And yet she plays the marimba in concerts all over the world, sometimes with an orchestra. She feels the vibrations in her feet. Just listen to this. I've got a great CD here if I can find it. Don't you underestimate the power of the human spirit. Just listen to how* **she greets the Millennium.** *Now remember she cannot hear a thing she is playing. Just listen to her rendering of* **Rag of Colts from the Sugar Factory.** *I just don't know whether Evelyn Glennie has a faith or not, but there's a place reserved for her at God's table.*

TERRY *Make a change from those Heavenly voices, Miss.*

EMMA *I'll ignore that. But you're right, Tracy, for most people hard of hearing, the loss of music is probably the most awful, awful thing. Then you've got to try and find something else to take its place. Maybe you can enjoy Art even more than those who can see and hear. You have got to nurture the senses that God's given you. And if you try real hard, God will help you along the way. There's folks that have got ears to hear with and eyes to see with, but they have never heard of Johan Sebastian Bach, and they've never seen a Botticelli. They are the ones that are really deprived.*

TRACY *Do you think music makes for a better world, because it's holy?*

EMMA *It's better for the people who listen to it and enjoy it, but they won't necessarily be better people. But I firmly believe that it does help to make a country that's good to be in.*

Now let's round this lesson off with two pieces of fine spiritual music. It's appropriate that one comes from my part of the world, the other from yours. The voices you'll hear carry the spirit of God in them or, if you want, simply the human spirit. Take your pick. Either way enjoy, enjoy. First my childhood hero, Paul Robeson, singing that famous spiritual **Deep River.**

And to finish, just listen to this: **Hallelujah Chorus from Handel's Messiah.**

TRACY *Wow*

EMMA *You guys will never be alone in life when you have found music.*

Author's note

Spirituality defies definition. If you believe in a Universal Creator, it is very personal when you suggest that a piece of music has been touched by God. If you have no such belief, again it is a personal matter whether you feel that a particular piece of music radiates the human spirit. As you read this scene, feel free to put yourself in Emma Kirk's place, and enjoy supplying your own choice.

Scene 5

Office of the Director of Education

There is a desk and chair in one corner, and also a round table with 4 chairs.

David Harding is joined first by SEN Officer, Gerry Thompson.

DAVID *Come on in.*

GERRY *Many thanks.*

DAVID *I thought we should have a word first.*

GERRY *Do you think we are going to have a problem.*

DAVID *I don't think so. Margaret's all for Inclusion. She has to be really. No career prospects at all if you row against the tide.*

GERRY *So you think she'll cooperate.*

DAVID *If we play our cards right, yes. But I'm going to have to rely on the two of you to work out the detail. It really is your job not mine. But I'll back you up and you know the regional office will back you up too. Do whatever's necessary to see it through.*

GERRY *I do have some thoughts and I'll talk to Margaret about them.*

DAVID *I'll stay for the first part of our meeting and then leave you to it. I actually do have another meeting to go to. One other thing. I thought I could call up some reinforcements for you. The School is one LEA governor short. There's a retired NHS hospital manager who understands our problem. He wants to do the very best for kids with special needs but within an Inclusive environment. The NHS cannot service both Mainstream schools and Special Schools. Something has got to give. Human resources are finite and money is finite as well. Anyway, his name is John Lavers and I've asked him to pop in this afternoon as well. He can't stay long, but we can have a few words with him as well as with Margaret.*

(Knock on the door and Margaret Williamson comes in. During this scene Margaret feels a tension headache coming on and puts her hand up to her right temple to try to ease it.)

MARGARET *Not too late I hope?*

DAVID *Not at all. Take a seat. I do hope that I haven't taken you away from anything important.*

MARGARET *Everything's important at Brighouse.*

DAVID *I've asked Gerry to join us this afternoon. He and you have a little job to do. I've also asked John Lavers to drop in as well. He's just retired from hospital management and I think he can help. We are suggesting that he fills the LEA vacancy on your governing body.*

MARGARET *That sounds really good. We've wanted a link with Health for a long time.*

DAVID *Can I come to the point of our meeting?*

MARGARET *Sure.*

DAVID *It's a bit delicate. Can I rely on your discretion?*

MARGARET *I suppose - how delicate?*

DAVID *Well, really very delicate.*

MARGARET *Oh dear. You had better break it to me.*

DAVID *You know we need to close your school.*

MARGARET *I was hoping that the parents might have persuaded you to change your mind.*

DAVID *Their campaign wasn't a waste of time. It forced us to address the closure much more seriously than we otherwise would have done. We do realise that we have got to work very hard to make sure that your kids don't lose out. We can't afford to have a hundred angry parents on our back. I gather, by the way, that you think that more than half of your roll could do well in mainstream schools.*

MARGARET *Yes, if you prepared properly for them…. trained the staff to take them… .put an end to bullying … and give them the attention and the time they need.*

DAVID *We are going to do all of that, aren't we Gerry?*

GERRY *Yes that's in hand.*

MARGARET *You going to stop bullying? Have you read how much there is of it today? One in four kids, and who gets bullied? The most vulnerable. Every time you fail, bullying may blight the entire life of one of our youngsters. Do you realise that? For them it's not just a learning experience that all kids have to go through, you know. It can be a life sentence, Gerry. And when you know the number of attempted suicides in youngsters every year, it can be a short life too.*

GERRY *We are tackling it, Margaret. We know we have to.*

DAVID *We certainly do, for the kids' sake, and to persuade parents to go along with us. We have to have parents on our side, not on our backs. Believe me.*

GERRY *That's what we are talking about today. We have a sort of plan.*

DAVID *I'll come straight to the point. We want you to sell the closure of the School to parents and staff.*

MARGARET *Last time you asked me to back you up. Now you're asking me to do the whole job for you. The answer is no, definitely no.*

DAVID *Things have moved on since last time.*

MARGARET *What things?*

GERRY *We're better prepared. We've listened to your parents.*

MARGARET *Come on Gerry, you've written a few more concept papers.*

GERRY *That's not fair. Training for special needs has started in mainstream schools. Headteachers say they are prepared.*

MARGARET *They say what you want them to say. Look, I gave a lot of thought to this last year. I don't want to take sides in this. It's not my job. It's yours, not mine. It's yours. I'm just not prepared to do it for you. I can't betray my own school like that, not after the parents' campaign to keep it open. I can't and you shouldn't be asking me to.*

DAVID *Margaret, we are asking you to face the reality of the situation, and get parents to do the same.*

GERRY *How many did your roll drop by last year?*

MARGARET *Nine.*

GERRY *I hear its going to drop by another fourteen this year.*

MARGARET *It certainly will if you keep kids from being admitted.*

GERRY *We don't stop them. We help them go to mainstream schools. And it will get worse for you. With fewer pupils and our new banding scheme you are going to have to face some big budget cuts. There'll have to be redundancies. Or you'll simply lose staff as they look around for greater job security and advancement. And you won't be able to replace them. I don't know whether you've heard but your Music Teacher, Emma Kirk's her name, yes*

MARGARET *Yes*

DAVID *She'll shortly be leaving you for a regional appointment. It's a big step up for her.*

MARGARET *Something tells me you're way ahead of me here.*

DAVID *If we are, you'll soon catch up.*

MARGARET *The school is to wither on the vine?*

DAVID *Your words not mine. But it's got to happen anyway. You must see that.*

MARGARET *I do, all too clearly.*

DAVID *Will you help us? if you do, you'll end up with a much better chance of a headship elsewhere. There's one coming up in the next couple of years in Grovewood Comprehensive School. And there may be a job for your English teacher too. We do have a little influence in these things, you know.*

MARGARET *I really don't know whether I'm hearing you right. Are you seriously saying that you want me to betray my kids?*

DAVID *Not betray them. Look to their best long term interests.*

GERRY *We don't want another public confrontation between the school and the LEA. That's no good for anyone, is it? And it can't be good for you or your colleagues. It just sours everything when we are trying to pull together and get things right for your kids.*

DAVID *Sometimes you have to be cruel to be kind.*

MARGARET *You admit that you're being cruel.*

DAVID *But I am trying to be kind. Look, you have said that half your School roll would fit into mainstream.*

MARGARET *Yes, if you can get it right for them*

DAVID *That's what we have to do.*

GERRY *That's our job now.*

MARGARET *But you haven't really started it.*

DAVID *It's what we have to do. OFSTED will be on our backs if we don't.*

MARGARET *I thought OFSTED was interested in standards and wouldn't like what you are suggesting.*

DAVID *You misread it. They'll turn a blind eye to it. They won't put a black mark against you or your school while this is going on. And when they inspect us they're only interested in whether we are delivering government policy and meeting government targets. That's the way that things get done.*

MARGARET *And people get done.*

GERRY *Margaret, just look two years ahead. Fewer kids. Less money. Fewer staff. Do you think you personally, never mind the School, can face an OFSTED inspection.*

MARGARET *I'll have to if that's what the parents want.*

DAVID *Look, we're all in the same boat. Can't you see that? If you lose half your school, do you really think that you can deliver the national curriculum to the rest?*

MARGARET *It wouldn't be easy.*

DAVID *It wouldn't be possible. And meanwhile you'll have a battle royal on your hands. The parents will be on your back and on ours, and don't think you can escape the backwash. You'll still need another job sometime. You must see that you will have queered your own pitch. People will be looking for reasons not to appoint you. You must see the danger of that.*

MARGARET *I haven't much alternative then?*

DAVID *None.*

MARGARET *Tell me, am I a mouse in a trap or a rat leaving a sinking ship?*

DAVID *Neither, you're just doing the job you're paid to do, like everyone else. When you are employed by the State you're not paid to ask questions. In particular, you're not paid to ask yourself any questions. That's not part of your job description, and it's incompatible with Health and Safety Regulations.*

MARGARET *When you're employed by the State, you don't have to be brain dead but it helps. Of course this is how the Germans and the Russians learnt how to survive their little dictatorships. Can I have a glass of water please?*

DAVID *Are you okay?*

MARGARET *Yes, just a little problem I have to live with.*

(David fetches a glass and hands it over. It slips between them and spills.)

MARGARET *I'm so sorry.*

DAVID *No. it was my fault.*

(He refills the glass)

MARGARET *Thanks.*

(Margaret slowly swallows three pills)

MARGARET *These usually help. Would you excuse me for a minute?*

DAVID *Sure. Take your time.*

(Margaret leaves the room)

DAVID *I just hate doing this.*

GERRY *You know it's best for everyone in the long run, including Margaret.*

DAVID *I guess I'm just a bit old fashioned. The world's changing, not always for the better.*

GERRY *But that's the point here. We are trying to change it for the better. I really think you did a great job there. She'll go along with us. You see.*

DAVID *I think I could do with a glass of water. I wish it was gin! No pills, though.*

(Gerry fills a glass and hands it over - Margaret enters the room)

DAVID *Look, don't think I don't respect you. And don't think you're alone with this sort of problem. It's the same for all of us. The Minister puts it about that we are responsible for school closures, but asks OFSTED to make sure that we close them. Brownie points if we do, a bad report if we don't. It's the system. Now we need good headteachers like you. But I do need to make sure you stay within the system, don't work against it. Are you going to help us?*

MARGARET *Give me the weekend to think it over. Please.*

DAVID *No, I'm not going to do that. For your sake. You'll only prolong the agony of making the decision you know you have to make. I'm sure we've said nothing you haven't already thought about, thought about a lot..*

MARGARET *I register a protest on behalf of the Governors and the parents.*

DAVID *But you'll go along with us?*

MARGARET *I will. Yes, yes I will. But in my heart you know I am saying no, no I won't. You understand that, don't you?*

DAVID *I do. I am very grateful. I know it goes against the grain. What we want is very simple. Break the news to governors that you're going to run short of money next year, and there'll have to be redundancies. Then tell them that we have no alternative but to close the school and you recommend they go along with it. We'll then call a parents' meeting, and you'll break the news to them. After that we'll put the formal procedures in motion and take the proposal to the School Organisation Committee.*

MARGARET *Simple for you. Not quite so simple for me.*

DAVID *We'll give you some reinforcements. I'm going to introduce you to John Lavers this afternoon.. He's just retired as an NHS Hospital Manager and he's got some free time. He does want to help with the transitional arrangements to make sure your kids get the right medical care after the school closes. He also sees the need to close the School from an NHS* standpoint. *They are strapped for cash and expertise - they just can't serve patients in special schools and in mainstream. Something has to give.*

(Knock on the door and John Lavers enters)

JOHN *Can I come in?*

DAVID *Yes do. Just the right moment. Can I introduce you to Margaret Williamson, head of Brighouse? You know Gerry.*

DAVID *She is one of our really good special school heads. Not all of them understand the imperative of Inclusion these days. She does. She knows you have to push it along.*

JOHN *From a health point of view it's very important you don't spend too much time progressing it. We just can't support both special schools and mainstream schools. You know Brighouse is probably getting more than its fair share today. It's not fair and equitable to other special needs kids. We do need to sort it.*

DAVID *Will you help? We don't want the kids to lose out, and helping us address their health needs must be good use of your time.*

JOHN *I'll wear that.*

DAVID *So we can co-opt you to the governing body of Brighouse.*

JOHN *If Margaret is happy about it, certainly.*

MARGARET *How can I object?*

DAVID *Good. I'll sort out the paperwork.*

DAVID *Look, I've got another meeting to go to and I think you have too John. I take it you'll go along with our thoughts here, Margaret? Long term it must be good for everyone. I'll leave you and Gerry to sort things out. Do come back to me if you need to. Forgive me if I go.*

MARGARET *Yes, I'm with you. Heaven save me.*

GERRY *We do support our friends, you know.*

MARGARET *Thank you very much.*

DAVID *It'll be alright. We'll make sure of it. And I think you will find the grass is greener on the other side of the fence.*

MARGARET *Okay Gerry, tell me what you have in mind.*

(David Harding and John Lavers leave the room)

MARGARET *This will be the death of me. I really don't like to let myself down, never mind anyone else.*

GERRY *It's in a good cause, you know that.*

MARGARET *So what have you got in mind.*

GERRY *You know the arguments for Inclusion. Recite them … with conviction.*

MARGARET *It sounds so easy. Good teachers are going to lose their jobs.*

GERRY *Oh, come on. If they are good we'll find them new ones, and their expertise with special needs will go to mainstream schools. That's where it needs to be now. It'll help your kids when they go there. There's a nice thought for you to finish with.*

MARGARET *Yes, I suppose it is.*

GERRY *Great.*

MARGARET *Just one final thought. What happens when the school is actually being closed? I just can't face that. Some of my parents are not going to like that.*

GERRY *A little sick leave perhaps?*

MARGARET *That will not be difficult.*

GERRY *Well, you heard the Director. There's an exit strategy for you all ready when you need it.*

MARGARET *I bet he won't put it in writing. I bet he won't put any of this in writing.*

GERRY *You can't expect that.*

MARGARET *What have I let myself in for?*

GERRY *A six month break, if you play your cards right.*

MARGARET *I must go and drown myself in porridge. That seems the right place for me to be.*

GERRY *Keep out of the soup.*

Scene 6

Head teacher's living room

There is a small couch and two easy chairs, CD player and a bookcase. A bottle of wine is on the table with a glass.

Margaret Wiliiamson is on her own to begin with. She is joined by Joan Errington who lets herself in.

MARGARET *Help yourself to a glass of wine.*

JOAN *Yes, I will*

MARGARET *It's been a hell of a bad week, one of my worst downers for a long time. Tommy Dixon died. He was only thirteen. What a great kid. Everyone knew he was on borrowed time. His friends were fantastic. Then Johnny Rutherford's mum wanted more speech and language therapy for her child, but just not available. You can't produce it out of the hat, can you? I lost my cool, and she lost hers. She said she'd report me to the Governors. I can really do without that. Then another parent, Terry James's father, said she wanted to report Emma to the Governors, and we can all do without that too.*

JOAN *Emma? I thought everyone loved our music teacher?*

MARGARET *Not this time. She's been propagating her Pentecostal ideas in her music lessons. That's what Mr. James alleges. He says he's an atheist and he objects. Then for good measure he said that if he was a Christian he'd also object. Emma believes God is a woman and he said that's heresy.*

JOAN *Poor Emma. She can't win either way. Did you discuss it with her?*

MARGARET *Yes, of course I did. She insisted that she was not propagating her faith, she was just describing it, and was entitled to her opinions. She said the Fawzis were very interested in her religion and dad's a Sikh. I think they both follow the Sikh faith³⁴Well I had to tell her she lived in an age of political correctness, and she had to keep her opinions to herself.*

JOAN *I'll bet Emma didn't go along with that.*

75

MARGARET *She did not, and it got quite heated. We're supposed to be educating these kids, she shouted. They have to learn how to agree and how to disagree, and when. How can I teach them if you gag me? And she went out slamming the door. Then the 'phone rang. I had a really distraught mum complaining about the LEA. She's wanted her son admitted to this School for ages. The LEA will admit him to almost any other one. You wouldn't believe what her son's been doing - smearing his business all over the walls of the house. Sheer frustration if you ask me. I am sure we could do something for that boy. And that poor lady is having to deal with this all on her own.*

JOAN *Well that's the sort of thing that happens when the LEA decides to starve a school of pupils. Positively inhumane, if you ask me.*

MARGARET *I'm afraid that it is. The real problem is the LEA. And they actually want me to work with them to close the school ...to try and prove to the parents that the School just isn't viable, and that their kids would be better served in mainstream schools. I don't like letting the school down, but you can't fight them, can you? They are bound to win in the end whatever our parents say.*

JOAN *What do they want you to do?*

MARGARET *Just argue their case for them, the case for Inclusion. They think it will be more persuasive if I say it than if they do.*

JOAN *They're certainly not wrong about that.*

MARGARET *And they're going to make it easier for me. Easier! We are going to run short of money with falling rolls and budget cuts. There'll have to be redundancies. Everything I've worked for. My God. And I've got to applaud it. You know they even suggested I took down our Merit Board, where we show what our kids have achieved over the years. They said you can't live in the past.*

JOAN *That was our achievement as well as the kids.*

MARGARET *Well they don't want people reminded of it. Anyway, what's going to happen to our kids? Some will be alright, but I'll bet others won't be.*

It's not surprising that I have migraine during the day and Insomnia at night. And pills as and when.

If I am a good girl, the LEA has promised me another headship after this school closes. They didn't use the word promise, mind you. But they can work these things. They can work them both ways, of course. They write the references. And they help the other school read them. You can probably get a job there too if you want it.

JOAN *Did they say that?*

MARGARET *Yes. Knew it probably would sweeten the pill. Don't say they are not thoughtful about our needs*

JOAN *When they want to be.*

MARGARET *And we have to be thoughtful about their needs also when they want us to be.*

JOAN *And their needs are very clear*

MARGARET *Yes, to get more children into mainstream schools, saying they have a right to it.*

JOAN *Some people think that rights grow on trees. Just pass a law and you've planted another tree.*

MARGARET *Weeping willows, more like.*

JOAN *Trees or people?*

MARGARET *Politicians are all for human rights, but when it comes to delivering them, ah that's another matter. There are too many social engineers in politics. They think that all you have to do to change society is to pass another law. You know, human rights sometimes are just dreams, very beautiful dreams, but dreams..*

JOAN *Yes, if only it was easy to turns those dreams into reality.*

MARGARET *And when you wake up from your dream, what do you find? Your social engineer has put square pegs into round holes with Araldite.*

JOAN *That is the nub of it. Some people just don't realise that one person's right can become another person's restriction.*

MARGARET *That's so true. They gave me no choice. They really didn't. The Government wants schools like ours closed. They think it'll save money which it won't. They pass the buck to the local authorities to do their dirty work for them and the local authority passes the buck to me. God, what a lousy world.*

JOAN *I can see what's going on. They don't want another losing confrontation with parents at all costs.*

MARGARET *You know what I feel like? I feel like a lump of plasticine, a little lump of plasticine that they have twisted in to a shape of their own choosing.... (Pause).... Give me a hug, Joan, I must tell you there is one other thing that's happened this week that I found personally very upsetting.*

JOAN *What's that?*

MARGARET *I heard a member of staff talk about Queen Margaret, and I suddenly realised that she was talking about me. I could do without that.*

JOAN *We could both do without that*

(They snuggle up together on the couch)

MARGARET *I think I know the answer.*

JOAN *What?*

MARGARET *I'll resign.*

JOAN *That's a silly thing to do.*

MARGARET *No, it's not. It's the only thing to do.*

JOAN *Just put that idea right out of your head.*

MARGARET *Don't you understand. I'm pig sick of this job. And I'm pig sick of the world we're living in. Every damn thing is a cynical charade, and I'm now given a lead role.*

JOAN *If everyone who didn't like their job resigned, there'd be a hell of a lot of vacancies.*

MARGARET *(Begins to cry) Don't you understand, I just can't do it any longer. I can't look kids in the face. I can't look my staff in the face, or the governors. And, what's more, I can't look myself in the face either.*

JOAN *You must.*

MARGARET *I can't.*

JOAN *What about us?*

MARGARET *What about us? It won't make any difference if I'm not here.*

JOAN *Of course it will make a difference. But anyway it's a waste. You're a wonderful teacher and a wonderful head. You can't give all that up. What about your pension? What are you going to live on? What will you do with yourself?*

MARGARET *I'll find something. I won't be the first teacher to throw in the towel. Now will I?*

JOAN *Look, whoever takes your place will do what you've said you'd do, and probably without any conscience at all. What on earth are you going to gain?*

MARGARET *My conscience.*

JOAN *Oh, come on. That's self indulgence.*

MARGARET *Self Indulgence. Self Indulgence. Oh my god. How can you say that to me? You of all people. What a horrid thing to say. I don't think you understand me at all. I want out. I want out altogether. Out, out, out.*

JOAN *You're just trying to make a martyr of yourself.*

MARGARET *If that's the best thing you can say you'd better go.*

JOAN *Oh, be sensible.*

MARGARET *Go ... Please go.*

JOAN *I just hope and pray you'll come to your senses. In a year's time all this will be a bad dream.*

MARGARET *Just leave me alone. Leave me alone.*

(Joan exits with her head down)

Scene 7

Meeting of the Finance Committee

In the Head teacher's room There is a desk and chair in one corner and a number of easy chairs around the rest of the room.

Margaret Williamson is present already.

EILEEN *Can I come in?*

MARGARET *Of course*

EILEEN *How are you?*

MARGARET *Is that a serious question?*

EILEEN *Actually it is. I have heard you're on a bit of a short fuse at the moment.*

MARGARET *I am getting pig sick of this.*

EILEEN *Come on, what's the problem?*

MARGARET *I hate all this talking behind my back. If someone has a complaint why don't they come and tell me?*

EILEEN *Did you call a parent a silly bitch?*

MARGARET *I did and I didn't.*

EILEEN *What do you mean by that? You either did or you didn't.*

MARGARET *Johnny Rutherford's mum comes in to see me demanding, yes demanding speech and language therapy for her kid. You know it's in short supply. You can't just switch it on like a tap, can you? Well, she kept on demanding it. Needless to say we got nowhere slowly. She left the room. And after she left, I said "silly old bitch". She must have heard me, and now everyone seems to know about it. I have a teacher friend in another school, you know Molly Brown, you've met her here. She'd heard about it. God. What a world.*

FRANK *Am I interrupting?*

MARGARET *No. We're finished what we were talking about. Leastways I hope we're finished.*

EILEEN *Yes we are*

FRANK *I'm glad to get away from my desk today. Everyone wants printing jobs done yesterday.*

EILEEN *Are you sure they shouldn't have been done yesterday?*

FRANK *I am not really complaining. I am only too pleased the work's there to do. You know even though everyone seems to have ink jet printers and laser printers and the latest editing programmes, they still come to me with their work.*

EILEEN *Paperless society! I know just one person who tries that with his electronic notepad.*

MARGARET *The DfES has a forest all of their own for the wood pulp.*

(Enter Tommy Jeffers, Jilly James and John Lavers)

JILLY *Hi*

TOMMY *Hello, everyone. I hope this isn't going to be a long meeting. I've got a very busy schedule of meetings to clerk today.*

MARGARET *I don't think so. I just want to flag up a few things.*

FRANK *Well let's begin then. Can I welcome you John. We'll regularise your presence on this committee later. I know my colleagues will be delighted you're joining us, LEA appointed, yes? (John Lavers nods) I am sure they will want you on our Finance Committee. It's really great building bridges between health and education, especially for us. And we can tap into your know-how. Thank you Margaret for setting it up.*

MARGARET *Don't give me the credit, chair. It was the LEA.*

FRANK *Well, well, caveat danaos. Sorry. Your experience is going to be invaluable and your network. For a start you can help us understand LEA bookkeeping.*

JOHN *Thank you for the welcome. There's only one thing you need to understand about their bookkeeping and that is that you are not supposed to understand it.*

EILEEN *If we knew what they knew, they wouldn't want to know. The more we know what they know, the more we'll interfere.*

JOHN *They do like to keep control of their territory.*

EILEEN *Are you saying that they think we're invaders?*

FRANK *No, they think we'd be intruders, not invaders, on their territory, and on yours too Margaret.*

MARGARET *That's not very nice. I really do try to keep you in the picture.*

FRANK *Enough…. Let's start our meeting. Margaret where are we up to?*

JILLY *You mean what are we up to?*

MARGARET *What do you mean by that? Oh forget it. Things are okay, this year at any rate. Next year there could be a problem.*

EILEEN *Tell us something we don't know.*

MARGARET *I mean it. The Authority called a meeting of special heads to discuss how they were going to divide the pot next year. Unfortunately I missed it. I had the most terrible migraine that day. I am told they all agreed to alter the ground rules. They have changed the banding requirements, you* know the way they work out how much each school gets to meet the needs of their pupils, and we have drawn the short straw.

EILEEN *I am not sure that your colleagues are your friends.*

MARGARET *You have no friends in this game. They are all a bit jealous of our success. The local paper always seems to be reporting things that our kids have done.*

JILLY *Why shouldn't it? We are the best special school out there..*

MARGARET *We may have to pay a price. I'm having a word with the Director about what it all means for us.*

TOMMY *I don't think you'll get anywhere. The wheels are already turning.*

MARGARET *You mean grinding.*

EILEEN *I hope they are not grinding us.*

TOMMY *You always seem to come through, don't you?*

MARGARET *Anyway, this year wasn't easy. Next year is going to be difficult. It's our falling rolls. We've a big cohort leaving this summer, and no-one taking their place. It's going to hit our budget. We may get some money from Europe, but I think that's drying up. And we might get some more franchise money. I'll try to keep you posted.*

FRANK *Can you give me some idea of the figures in all this.*

MARGARET *It's too soon.*

FRANK *We need more pupils, that's the long and short of it. You should raise this personally with the Director.*

EILEEN *We've tried, Frank. He says parents are simply choosing other schools.*

JOHN *There's nothing we can do about it, so don't even think about it.*

FRANK. *Does that cover everything? If it does, can I go?*

EILEEN *I think we must all go. The Head's got work to do.*

MARGARET *That's certainly what I want people to think.*

EILEEN (leaving the room) *Relax a bit, if you can.*

MARGARET *Who can relax when you're a teacher?*

Scene 8

Music Room – a letter to the PM

Terry, Philippa, Tracy and Harry are in the room. Terry is strumming a guitar. Tracy is tapping a steel drum.

HARRY *Have you heard the story of the fella applying for a job?*

TRACY *No, go on.*

HARRY *Well he asked the boss what the hourly rate was.*

TRACY *Yes*

HARRY *And the boss said ten pounds an hour.*

TRACY *So?*

HARRY *Not good enough for him. Asked him what the chance was for promotion.*

TRACY *Good on him. Showed he had ambition.*

HARRY *Well the boss said, if he was good and if he performed well, after three months he'd get fifteen pounds an hour.*

TRACY *Yes, so?*

HARRY *So the boss said did he want the job and the fella said yes he did. Then the boss asked when he could start. The fella said in three months.*

(Enter Johnny)

JOHNNY *What have I missed*

TRACY *A stupid story.*

TERRY *Been down to the Westborough Post?*

86

JOHNNY *Yes, this time been at the sports desk.*

TERRY *Did you cover our great win over the Rovers?*

JOHNNY *I did. Wrote it up for them.*

HARRY   *Four nil to us. What a match.*

JOHNNY *My first report.*

HARRY *It's a beginning. That's great. Congratulations.*

TRACY *There some more good news on the school grapevine. Susan's got into Bristol to read History and David Wilson's got into the Post Office.*

PHILIPPA *He can deliver my letter for me.*

HARRY *What letter?*

PHILIPPA *To the Prime Minister. Special wheel chair delivery to 10 Downing Street. It'll make a good picture in your newspaper.*

HARRY *I wouldn't waste my time. My dad's written lots of letters all over the place. Never seemed to get anywhere at all.*

PHILIPPA *Well I'm writing to the Prime Minister. He said Education, Education, Education and I am taking his word for it.*

HARRY *He could have said rhubarb, rhubarb, rhubarb so far as this school is concerned.*

PHILIPPA *That's the point of my letter. I am telling him he should visit this school and meet us.*

HARRY *There's no votes in it.*

PHILIPPA *There will be soon enough. Do you want to hear what I have written?*

HARRY *Yea, go on, tell us.*

PHILIPPA *"Dear Mr. Prime Minister*

I am writing to invite you to visit my school. I am writing to you personally because you should know what pupils like me think about where we should be taught. And you should see for yourself just how much we will lose if this school is closed. My parents told me this could still happen, even though all our parents said that they wanted it kept open.

My childhood was a happy one, but difficult at the same time. When you are in a wheel chair and all your friends have been walking straight away, it clicks you're different.

I first went to a primary school but I was called "old wheelie bin" there and that was not very pleasant. Some friends of mine were called "spackers." Then I came here to Brighouse. They gave me real enthusiasm for living. Brighouse does not take or give the easy option. It pushes everyone to the full and then pushes some more. They pushed me academically and physically even though I am in a wheel chair. I've competed three times in Great North Runs, and I went to the Athens ParaOlympics with two of my friends. I won a Silver medal, and my friend a Gold.

And I am planning to get my GCSE's and word processing qualifications.

And I also play in the Tin Pan Ally Steel Drum Band. We have gigs every week and give a lot of pleasure to a lot of people and especially to ourselves.

Children like me don't want to be social experiments. We have got one chance and the staff here know just how to make it a real one.

If you could just spare the time to come down to our school, and look into the eyes of the children and ask them where they want to be, I personally guarantee you won't want us to go anywhere else.

I may not be a voter today. But I soon will be.

Yours sincerely,
Philippa Jones,
Pupil Brighouse Special School
Westborough."

JOHNNY *A great letter. Couldn't do better myself. Front page stuff.*

PHILIPPA *Front page in the Westborough Post?*

JOHNNY *No, you clown. The school newspaper.*

PHILIPPA *Do you think that the Westborough Post might report it?*

JONNY *They might. I'll try them.*

(Enter Emma)

EMMA *Hey you lot, why are you not practising for Saturday. You don't need me all the time.*

TRACY *Yes we do. We'd be absolutely lost without you.*

EMMA *I just hope that isn't true. Come on 'Onward Christian Soldiers…' Mind you I'm not sure if it's safe to play that today.*

HARRY*I don't mind as long as we play some of my Indian music too.*

EMMA *We sure will. That's a promise. We'll listen to Ravi Shankar on his sitar next time. I've got a CD of 'Full Circle'. Great music. He got a Grammy award for it.*
Come on. Let's be real daring. 'Onward Christian soldiers…'

Scene 9

Head teacher's living room

Margaret Williamson is stretched out on couch, her arm touching the floor. A glass is beside her. Joan Errington lets herself in but leaves the door ajar. She thinks Margaret is dead. She has taken overdose. Joan thinks that she may have herself have contributed to this by walking out. She may even have been a bit selfish in arguing with her.

JOAN (Screaming and shaking Margaret) *Oh my God* , (picks up 'phone) *I should have seen it coming.... Ambulance quickly ....Joan Errington ... I'm at 12 Oakley Way, Westborough, W13 5 NX... 07524 39102 ... A lady here ... Margaret Williamson ... seems to have taken an overdose ... please come as quickly as you can.... Yes ... she's still breathing but I can't wake her. ...Yes*

JOAN (dials another number) *Oh, Eileen. So glad I've found you. Joan, Joan Errington. Terrible thing here. It looks as though Margaret's tried to take her own life.*
She's still breathing. Seems to be in a coma. .... Yes I've tried ..... No, I can't wake her. I have called 999. Maybe the medics will save her. She's left me a note. Can I read it?
"My dearest Joan. I am so sorry that you will probably be the one to find this letter and what's left of me. You may think that our long friendship and all the things we have shared together deserved a better fate. Please don't think ill of me. You know about my black moods. They have been getting blacker and blacker these last few weeks. Anti-depressants haven't helped. You've tried, I know. And there's my terrible headaches too. Do try and explain to people,. Please don't say anything against me. I am sure you won't. In recent months it has been just so very difficult - so bloody, bloody difficult - to come into work with a smile, look colleagues in the face, encourage them to do their job. I'm not made of stone. Think of the good times. There have been some great times, you and I and the school. Good bye, my love, Margaret."
She has been treated for depression on and off for some time. .... Yes, of course you would know.... It was pretty well managed most of the time and she was a great teacher, brilliant with the kids. .... Yes... Tell me a teacher that isn't depressed at times.. ... Take her own life? Maybe it was just a cry

90

for help. She knew I was coming,   but I got here a bit earlier than planned …. It's your guess. … Anyway that's why she's been on such a short fuse recently…. Yes, she has done a few strange things recently…She'd even thought about resigning. I could have been more sympathetic. … No I know I mustn't blame myself. … Yes, we all tried to protect her (Ringing bells get nearer then stop)…. *Here's the ambulance. See you first thing tomorrow morning. Do hope she pulls through. … Yes I am afraid it is a lose…lose situation for her now. But even if they're in time, she'll find it difficult to make it back to her job. Just got to hope. I do so hope. You know we are very close…. Most people do know. This is so awful, so god damn awful.* (Ambulance men enter.)

ACT TWO

Scene I

In the Directors Room

David Harding is joined by Gerry Thompson.

DAVID *Come*

GERRY *Morning*

DAVID *Certainly not good morning. Isn't it horrific news about Margaret Williamson?*

GERRY *God, yes. Who would have thought she would do that?*

DAVID *The latest news I have is that they've brought her round. You know I could never have lived with myself if they hadn't.*

GERRY *Me too. We talked about her getting six months' sick leave but not this way.*

DAVID *I do hope it doesn't get into the press.*

GERRY *I am sure it won't. But it's around everywhere.*

DAVID *I don't want it to be thought it was because of anything we are doing.*

GERRY *I think quite a few people know she has a problem and is under medication for it.*

DAVID *Good. Now where do we go from here? You were suggesting that we call in our old friend Don Smithson.*

GERRY *Yes, I was.*

DAVID *I agree with you. He's a retired teacher, does odd jobs for us and he knows our ways. He could help us steer the school through some difficult times. I've invited him to drop in this morning to see us. Can you sell him to the school?*

GERRY *I am sure I can. They haven't a deputy, so they should be very grateful for an experienced stand in. But we'll have to put him in the picture.*

DAVID *Yes we will. He's pretty savvy so I don't think there'll be a problem. Ah talk of the devil.*

(Don Smith knocks and enters)

DON *Morning all. Sorry I'm a bit out off puf. Why on earth did someone put the Council Offices on top of the one and only hill in Westborough?*

DAVID *So the Council could look down on the good citizens of Westborough.*

DON *And we could look up to them….. For my shopping.*

(Dumping a rucksack and helmet on a chair)

I've just heard the terrible news. Is Margaret okay?

DAVID *I am pleased to say she is. They've brought her round.*

DON *I am so pleased. I've got a lot of time for her. And she's a great teacher even if she is a bit up and down at times. I hope you haven't been putting too much pressure on her.*

DAVID *It's a bit complicated. That's why we need your help.*

DON *I am not sure whether I am best called a plumber's mate or an organ grinder's monkey, but I am here to oblige.*

DAVID *I'll try to explain. You know we've been trying to close Brighouse for some time.*

DON *And the parents have been a bit stroppy about it.*

DAVID *Yes, more than a little, and the governors too.*

DON *I followed it all in the press. You got a bit of a sore arse.*

DAVID *I suppose I have.*

DON *And you're going to try again.*

DAVID *You know us too well. But it is in a good cause, you know that.*

DON *And I suppose your lords and masters are telling you to get off your backside and sort it.*

DAVID *As a matter of fact they are, but don't say I said so.*

DON *So what do you want me to do?*

DAVID *Take over the school for six months, maybe a year.*

DON *Well, I've nothing on at the moment.*

DAVID *And we want you to sell the closure to the governors and the parents. It'll come better from you than from us.*

DON *I suppose that's what upset Margaret?*

DAVID *It didn't help. But she had a problem anyway. It's common knowledge.*

DON *I'll have to do your dirty work. What's new about that?*

DAVID *You may find the Governors a bit difficult.*

DON *And what's new about that either? They must know their place, that's my golden rule.*

DAVID *Well make sure you keep them in it if you can.*

DON *You're lucky. I was a very good slip catcher in my day.*

DAVID *And you were a canny spin bowler too if I remember. Didn't you once take seven wickets for thirty?*

DON *That was a very long time ago. Batsman said I had a very well disguised googly, not to mention a shooter with some wicked top spin.*

GERRY *I bet no-one said it wasn't cricket.*

(Gentle laughter)

DAVID *Look you and Gerry go off and he'll put you in the picture. Do tell everyone at the school how personally sorry I am about all this. And do assure them that I don't want the kids to suffer at all, not at all.*

GERRY *Director, you have a heart, even though you do keep it hidden from us some of the time.*

DAVID *I hope I have. I couldn't do this job if I didn't. Go on, get on your way both of you. Remember it's always darkest before the dawn.*

DON *The trouble is never, ever, ever comes the dawn. Bye.*

DAVID *Just watch that bicycle of yours. We certainly can't afford another of our head teachers risking life and limb..*

(Don collects his helmet and rucksack, and leaves the room with Gerry).

DAVID (picks up the " phone) *Would you try and get me James Harrington in London, please...... James. Glad I've caught you. I thought you should know. The head of Brighouse has tried to kill herself. .... No, mercifully not ... silly old what?.. I am not sure who is the silly old thing ... No, I haven't lost control .... Yes, I am upset ... and so should you be. It could have been a disaster. ... I agree it isn't. .. It's actually opportunistic. We are putting one of our own people into the school to head it up. .... Yes, I am sure the governors will go along with it. .... No I won't lose any sleep. ... Just thought you should know. Bye.*

And so he damn well should.

Scene 2

Emergency meeting of governors

Held in the staff room to agree on a temporary replacement for the head teacher, and to address financial problems.

(Tommy Jeffers is on his own. He is then joined by Eileen Winterton)

EILEEN *Hello, you here before everyone?*

TOMMY *Yes*

EILEEN *Bad business with Margaret.*

TOMMY *Sad business. Any idea how she is?*

EILEEN *She's conscious but still in hospital. They don't want to let her home yet. Have you ever come across a headteacher trying to take her own life before?*

TOMMY *Never. Have had pupils mind you trying to do it after they have been bullied, but never a teacher.*

EILEEN *Difficult to know why on earth she did it. You'd think being a head here was such a fulfilling job, the very last thing she's want to do would be to take an overdose.*

TOMMY *I am told she had some personal medical problems and bad migraines too. They said in the office she had cluster headaches.*

EILEEN *I don't think that's true, but recently she did certainly get bad migraines. I didn't think they were serious enough to make her take an overdose.*

TOMMY *There's no way you can know, is there?*

(John Lavers enters)

EILEEN *Welcome John. Sorry you join us at sad and difficult times.*

JOHN *I hope I can help.*

(Other governors enter with Gerry Thompson and sit round the table)

EILEEN *Hello everyone. Are we all here? Any apologies?*

TOMMY *We've had an apology from Vice Chair, Councillor Thomas. He's out of town and asked me to say how very sorry he is that he can't make this meeting.*

EILEEN *This, as you all know, is an emergency meeting. Thank you for coming at shorter notice than usual. There's just three items on the agenda, one our headteacher, two a temporary replacement and three the budget for next year. First I'd formally like to welcome John Lavers to this meeting. He's a new LEA appointed governor. He's just retired as an NHS Hospital Manager with some time on his hands. We've badly needed a link with the Health. Really glad you are joining us.*

JOHN *I do think Health and Education should work closely together especially when it comes to helping disabled children.*

EILEEN *I've also invited Gerry Thompson to be with us today. We have a situation arising from poor Margaret's attempt on her life - what's the latest there? Joan you probably know the latest.*

JOAN *Yes, I saw her in hospital yesterday. She's alright, but very weepy. She's certainly not well.*

EILEEN *It must have hit you hard.*

JOAN *It's hit everyone here very hard. I suppose me most of all. Yes.*

EILEEN *Well, it leaves a big hole to be filled. I've had a very short letter from Margaret. I think I should read it." I do apologise to everyone at the school. I am so very sorry. My doctors think that I should take some time away. They think six months. Could you possibly give me leave of absence for that* time? I've just got to avoid all stress for a time. Thanks if you can. Margaret Williamson."

FRANK *We've obviously got to go along with that.*

EILEEN *Yes. Does everyone agree?* (Nods all round). *I'll get a message back to her tomorrow and send her our very best wishes.* (Nods all round)*I thought that this might be the case and the LEA did too. They really have moved to help us. Anyway that's why I have asked Gerry to be with us. Gerry.*

GERRY *We are all very sad about Margaret too. The Director asked me to say how personally upset he is. He has asked me to put a suggestion to you. You have no deputy head, and you've got some difficult times ahead. There's a budget situation to deal with for a start.*

EILEEN *We've got to deal with that later this evening.*

GERRY *Yes. Anyway the Director thought that Don Smithson might help out. He's a retired headteacher and takes on assignments for us. He could be your acting headteacher if you wanted him.*

EILEEN *I knew that this was being suggested, and I got the Personnel Committee to meet Don and they recommend that we thank the LEA for their help and accept their suggestion. Don is actually here and can join us this evening if you like.*

(Nods all round)

EILEEN *Well that's agreed then. Would you ask Don to come in.*

(Frank brings in Don Smithson)

EILEEN *Come on in. You are very welcome. A gift from the gods I think.*

DON *A gift from the LEA.*

JILLY *We're not used to getting gifts from the LEA, sorry Gerry.*

FRANK *Not actually a gift. We are going to have to pay for your services.*

EILEEN *Not that we are not pleased to get them on that account. Do you know people here?*

DON *I know the teaching and care staff and quite a few parents. Hi Jilly. I have done some locum teaching in the school and I've just met the finance committee. And I know Tommy Jeffers of old. If there isn't a rule in the rule book, he'll write one for you.*

TOMMY *33 years experience gives you that facility.*

EILEEN *You know most of us then. There's Ahmed Fawzi, a Parent Governor and you know everyone.*

DON *Yes, indeed.*

GERRY *Would you allow me to go? I just want you to know that the LEA wants to be as helpful to you as it can be at this time. The Director will be very pleased to hear that you have taken Don Smithson on board. Good night everyone.*

(Exit Gerry)

EILEEN *Before we start the other part of our business this evening, there is one other piece of sad news for us. Emma has just been appointed regional adviser for music and leaves us at the end of term. Her enthusiasm for music is going to reach many more kids, and it is a great opportunity for her. I am sure we all wish her the very best in her new career.* (Nods all round)

JOAN *It is a fantastic opportunity for her. I think she really was pulled two ways.*

JILLY *There's weeping and wailing in the Band. They don't think it'll continue without her.*

JILLY *Where on earth are we going to find anyone else like her?*

FRANK *I am afraid we'll have to come to that later this evening.*

ANWAR *What does that mean?*

FRANK Just *wait a while and you'll understand.*

EILEEN *Well let's come to the second item on the agenda. Our budget for next year, who is going to speak to it?*

DON *Would you like me to? I am new to it but I can probably explain it to you.*

FRANK *Yes, please do. I've a contribution to make as Chair of Finance, but I'll save it till later.*

DON (Passing around a piece of paper) *This is our budget for next year. Margaret's been working on it with the LEA. It's been to your Finance Committee. I must tell you that they didn't like it, but they felt that they had to go along with it.*

ANWAR *What's this? Is our income down by one hundred and thirty thousand pounds?*

DON *Hold your horses.*

ANWAR *What's going on?*

DON *I haven't got my head round all of it, but I can understand a lot of it. If Margaret was here I am sure she would be able to explain it to you. The main problem is our shrinking school roll. We used to have over a hundred and twenty kids. Now we're under ninety, and going down.*

ANWAR *You're right going down. Down and out!*

DON *We'll come to that, one thing at a time please. First we have got to agree on a budget and we've got to cut our coat according to our cloth.*

ANWAR *Where's all our cloth gone? That's what I want to know.*

DON *There is an explanation. We've had a net loss of fourteen pupils, year on year, and the banding arrangements have gone against us as well this year. Margaret did her best but there was nothing she could do about that.*

She missed a meeting because of a migraine, but I'm told it wouldn't have made any difference.

FRANK *This is all because the LEA has starved us of pupils.*

JOHN *Are you sure it isn't just a sign of the times. Parents want their kids in mainstream schools and the LEA is helping them to get there. They have to place them there if they possibly can. And this is the result.*

FRANK *I wonder whether it is as simple as that.*

TOMMY *I do have to remind you, you do have to agree a budget this evening. Otherwise the school can't buy anything.*

DON *I'm afraid that it does mean some redundancies. We'll have to lose four members of staff. I've got to ask you to agree that.*

ANWAR *Where does the axe fall then? Who's for the chop?*

DON *At worst it's only three redundancies. You remember that Emma is leaving us.*

ANWAR *Don't tell us we can't replace her. Music's one of the great things about our school.*

DON *Maybe we can get some part time help. I can tell you something else. You won't find anyone as good as Emma even if we had the cash. Good music teachers are very hard to come by. I agree, though, we'll have to try to make some provision for music. You'll have to trust me on that.*

ANWAR *Who else are we going to lose?*

DON *We can't decide that tonight. We'll see if anyone wants voluntary redundancy, and if that doesn't solve it, there's a procedure we have to follow to decide who we have to make redundant. All you have to do tonight is to agree on the figures in the budget.*

JOAN *This whole thing reminds me of Orwell's 1984. These figures don't tell the whole story. You remember when O'Brien is interrogating Winston and* he quotes the Party slogan "Who controls the past controls the future: who controls the present controls the past'. The LEA controls the past, the present and the future don't they? And not us.

EILEEN *You're still pretty upset about Margaret?*

JOAN *Yes I am.*

EILEEN *We do have a decision to take.*

FRANK *As Chair of Finance I've got to ask you to approve the budget. I don't think we've any alternative.*

JOHN *I'll second that.*

EILEEN *Do we all agree?*

(Everyone nods)

EILEEN *It is agreed then.*

DON *There is one other matter the LEA has asked me to sound you out on.*

EILEEN *You did warn me. You'd better bring it up.*

DON *You can see the way our finances are going. I can't see them getting any better. In fact, they can only get worse. I don't know whether you've heard about the Law of Diminishing Returns. Well our returns are going to diminish, and we are just not going to be able to deliver the National Curriculum to our kids. We might be able to do it this year, but I worry about the next one.*

I think that this is what has so upset Margaret.

JOAN *Not the only thing.*

DON *I'm sure it was the main thing. Anyway, I know your parents fought to keep the school open - you really shook up the LEA and, off the record, rightly in my view. They hadn't done their homework. But at least you've forced them to think through their policies to make sure they work. That was well worth doing. Anyway, they tell me, they assure me that if the school closes …*

ANWAR *Don't say we're opening all that again?*

DON *We have to. Don't you see? As I say, if the school closes the Director personally assures you that your kids will not lose out. You've got to trust him. I think you can trust him. He doesn't want a hundred angry parents on his back if he lets you down. Now does he?*

FRANK *So what is he asking you to say to us?*

DON *He wants to take steps to close the school. He wants to call another meeting of parents and he wants you to support him. He also wants me to speak at the meeting. He wants to win over the parents this time and he doesn't want another confrontation. Councillors don't want it. It wouldn't be a good thing.*

JILLY *I've said nothing till now. I'm not good at finance. But I'm not going to go along with that. We've fought before, and we'll fight again. We'll fight them on the bloody beaches.*

JOHN *You'll only rub people up the wrong way if you do. It's going to happen because it's got to happen. Don's right. We can't deliver. And the less we deliver the less parents will want their kids to be here. And more staff will leave to save themselves. Another fight can't be the right thing.*

FRANK *I agree you can't fight them. But I think they've helped to set this thing up. I have been happy to contribute my time to a going concern, but I'm not going to be a party to a scuttling operation. That's not what I joined you to do. I'm afraid I've got to resign. I can make much better use of my time. Much better.*

EILEEN *Frank, I know you're upset. We're all upset. We could all say we resign. That really wouldn't help our kids, now would it? Do please reconsider.*

FRANK *Sorry Eileen*

JOHN *There's an old saying.....Act in haste. Repent at leisure.*

FRANK *I'm not the one to do the repenting. Sorry. You have my resignation, as from now.*

EILEEN *I can see you've made up your mind. Thank you for all you've done over the years, Frank. We all thank you for that.*

FRANK *Thank you. It's been a privilege to be a governor of this school. I'm just so sorry it has to end this way. I do wish you and the school the best, and the kids. Bye everyone.*

(Exit Frank)

EILEEN *I'm very sorry about that. I'm sure you would want me to write to Frank and thank him for the many years service he has given the school.*

(Everyone nods in agreement)

I'll get that letter off tomorrow.

JILLY *Well, I'm not resigning. I'm going to vote against closure. I couldn't face the other parents if I did. I just couldn't. What's going to happen to my Terry? He's already lost one year getting in here. I won't have him losing another. I won't have it.*

DON *Terry'll be fine. He's a great kid, a survivor. Some kids are, you know.*

JILLY *I'll give you that. But no thanks to the LEA, it's thanks to this school. What if he wasn't a survivor? What about the kids that aren't survivors? What about them? You tell me, does the LEA care about them?*

JOHN *I'm sure they do. They haven't an easy job getting it right for everyone.*

EILEEN *Joan, you've been very silent. What do you think? Where do the staff stand?*

JOAN *This has been the saddest few weeks of my life. This whole thing is rotten to the core. I could weep. I really could.*

EILEEN *I know. But what do you think we should do?*

JOAN *I can see the logic in what the Head says. But I can't bring myself to vote for closure. I may be a chicken. I'm going to abstain.*

ANWAR *I'm voting against. The LEA has a responsibility to keep this school open for kids like Harry. We've got the right to opt out of mainstream schools. It's their problem not ours.*

JOHN *Sometimes in life you've just got to make tough decisions. This is one of them. We've got to support the Head.*

EILEEN *I'm not going to put this to the vote. It's not an agenda item. If the LEA want to call a meeting of parents, they don't need our approval for that. And if they want you, Don, to present the case for closure we can't stop you doing that, if you are comfortable doing that.*

DON *I wish I had your unanimous support. But I understand where you come from over this. It's not an easy one. It'll give me no pleasure you know. None at all. I know what this school means to you. Believe me, I do.*

TOMMY *How do you want me to minute this?*

EILEEN *You don't need to record the discord. Just say that we have noted with regret - we can all say that - what the LEA wants to do - that they are going to call a meeting of parents - and that our head will be presenting the case for closure.*

DON *I'm just going to present the facts of the present situation as I see them.*

EILEEN *Yes. I know what you are saying. That I think brings our meeting to an end. Can I wish Don the very best good fortune as our new acting head, and can I ask you Joan to give our very best wishes to Margaret when you next see her. Tell her not to worry about anything at all.*

JOAN *I certainly will.*

EILEEN *No other business?*

ALL *No*

EILEEN *We'll meet again next month at the termly meeting.*

(People drift away from the meeting saying goodnight to each other. Eileen Winterton and Joan Errington are slow to leave)

EILEEN *Thanks for 'phoning me. Tell me about Margaret.*

JOAN *Please don't press me. Just say she's a casualty of the world we are living in.*

EILEEN *I worry about that. Especially this bit of it.*

JOAN *So do I. I said as much when I mentioned 1984.*

EILEEN *Surely it's not as bad as that?*

JOAN *It is, and it isn't... what is a free society these days? Do you remember Hamlet's advice to mad Ophelia? "Get thee to a nunnery." Yes, today, you are free to go to a nunnery or a monastery for that matter, if you can find one open. Or you can busk your way through life if you choose to. You are free to wrap yourself in a blanket on Hungerford Bridge and beg, with your dog along side of you. You are free to have Prozac on the NHS - or crack cocaine off it*

EILEEN *That's illegal.*

JOAN *But how many people turn a blind eye to it? What I am saying is that in one sense you are free, but if you want some of the goodies you have got to accept Big Brother. We live in a dependent society. We depend upon each other. There's nothing wrong in that. But we also depend upon the State, and far too many people are totally dependent on it.*

EILEEN *Yes, I'm afraid that's very true.*

JOAN *There's absolutely no discrimination here, is there? People at the top of the pile can be every bit as dependent on the State as people at the bottom – probably more so. They have more to lose, or to win. And the price you pay for the State's beneficence, you obey it or you comply with it. You toe the party line, or you keep your head down, right down below the parapet.*

EILEEN *I think I've got the message.*

JOAN *In one sense it's nothing new you know. We are all in a Club. What's the first rule in any Club? You play by the rules, and we don't write them.*

EILEEN *So you think Orwell got the future right?*

JOAN *It's certainly the way it's going. What is "Spin" if it's not another word for "New Speak"? Can you believe anything you are told these days? Take the words "'parental choice" or "parental preference". When parents are not to be allowed by Law to talk to a school where their children might go, or when the schools they are supposed to choose from don't exist, because they have been shut, democratically of course, but shut all the same, you might as well say "parental rhubarb".*

EILEEN *I'm afraid you're right.*

JOAN *And there's far, far too much politics in education.*

EILEEN *It has to be. The State provides the money.*

JOAN *Yes, but it keeps meddling. It should demand standards, but it shouldn't keep meddling and trying to control us all the time.*

EILEEN *Tell me, would you like to be a Head Teacher one day?*

JOAN *I would not. Too much pressure from too many sides. I wouldn't have wanted Margaret's job for all the money in the world.*

EILEEN *We do get it wrong, if that's the case. Teachers like you have so much to give.*

JOAN *We certainly do know how you get it wrong. It makes me feel so sick at times, especially now. You know when terrible things like this happen - you know I'm very, very close to Margaret - you really start to think. I'll give you a* strange thought. The word 'Equality' is at the root of a lot of our trouble. It's mucked up education for years. We are not all equal.

EILEEN No, that's heresy. Surely there's got to be equality of opportunity?

JOAN What does that actually mean? Don't you see? All kids are different, very different, and they need different kinds of opportunity. Fair play is what they all want, not equality. If kids are not given the opportunity that's right for them, especially ours, they won't be equipped to meet the challenge of the times. They won't be included in this cut throat world that's coming in fast. And this country needs them to be. That's what education should be about. Above all else, giving them that opportunity.

EILEEN It certainly is a rat race these days and a different kind of rat race from any before.

JOAN But a rat race you can't run away from. And it has got a good side to it, if you know where to find it. I'm sure none of this sadness would have happened to Margaret if people realised like we do that all kids have very different needs.

EILEEN Well, I'm afraid our old friend Karl Marx is still around in education. People are looking for that elusive level playing field, and with the proviso that no-one actually competes on it.

JOAN I agree. They are looking for solutions to the world's problems in the libraries of their minds, not in the classrooms of the real world.

EILEEN To coin a phrase, Marxism is the opium of the brainy classes, despite everything. And they hate globalisation too. But you can't turn the clock back. Those people shouldn't be looking for an old clock. They should be looking for a new compass.

JOAN. There's a price to be paid for using education as a social tool. The problem used to be private wealth and public squalor. Today, it is private stress and public unhappiness. Just look at poor Margaret and our parents... and me.

JOAN *You're right. Dust to dust and ashes to ashes, if we don't get it right. Margaret's clearly not the only one suffering from depression.*

EILEEN *Oh dear, I shouldn't have started all this. I really am sorry I encouraged you to sound off.*

JOAN *Don't apologise. I badly, badly needed it. I don't much like the world I see. I can't pretend I do. But I'll find a way of living through it. You've just got to.*

EILEEN *Our little discussion has probably been usefully cathartic for both of us. And it has helped me to understand.*

JOAN *We're all of us walking wounded, we are all casualties, not just Margaret. I must away.*

EILEEN *So must I. Thank you for your time. I do appreciate it.*

JOAN *Night night.*

EILEEN *Pleasant dreams*

JOAN *Where do you suggest I find them?*

EILEEN *Look, there's a lot wrong with this world. There always has been. There always will be. But there's an awful lot right as well, isn't there? You've just got to ride that roller coaster between the two. And try not to fall off.*

JOAN *I suppose so. See you again soon.*

Scene 3

One month later

In Margaret Williamson's living room, Margaret is listening to music in her chair. Joan Errington is in the kitchen.

(The door bell rings, and Joan answers it)

FRANK *Hello. Ok to come in?*

MARGARET *Sure, take a chair.*

FRANK How *are you?*

MARGARET *A bit better than I have been, and a little worse than I could be.*

JOAN *Come on. You're a good deal better.*

MARGARET *I needed to be, didn't I?*

FRANK *You gave us all a terrible shock.*

MARGARET *I am so sorry about that. That's why I wanted you to come this afternoon. I owed you an explanation.*

FRANK *We really didn't want that, you know.*

MARGARET *I'll explain, when Eileen arrives. I have invited her to come as well.*

FRANK *You really don't have to explain.*

MARGARET *Actually I do. Would you like a cup of coffee, or a cup of tea.*

FRANK *Coffee please.*

JOAN *Instant, alright?*

FRANK *Of course, milk and no sugar.*

(Joan goes to make coffee)

MARGARET *And how are you? I hear you resigned from the Governors.*

FRANK *Yes I did. I was pretty upset at everything - that the LEA still wants to close the school. The leopard doesn't change its spots, does it?*

MARGARET *You'll be a big loss. Couldn't you have seen your way to stay?*

FRANK *You know they say business is the survival of the fittest. It's certainly tough, and it's rough. And there's precious little sentiment, especially these days. But by and large there's trust. There has to be if you are playing the long game, and you want to be successful. You probably think I'm a bit old fashioned to say this.*

MARGARET *If you are, don't for heaven's sake, apologise for it.*

FRANK *I am. Remember I'm a Rotarian. You know what every Rotarian signs up to - high ethical standards in business and the professions as an opportunity to serve society - and I'm not alone, you know. There's over a million of us world wide. Now the trouble is I just cannot trust the LEA, and I can't trust politicians either, not these days. Others felt they had to try. I couldn't. I've got plenty to do in my own company anyway.*

MARGARET *So you're not thinking of retiring there.*

FRANK *No way. Cannot even slack off. I have two boys and neither want anything to do with it. They're afraid that more and more printing will go abroad.*

(Joan brings back coffee)

JOAN *What do your boys do?*

FRANK *Thanks. One is in IT, working in Bangalore. That's where he says all the action is. And the other is on a gap year in Africa. He doesn't know what he is going to do after that.*

(The door bell rings. Joan answers and welcomes Eileen)

EILEEN *I hope I am not late.*

JOAN *No, just learning a bit about Frank's family. Coffee or tea?*

EILEEN *Coffee, black please.*

(Joan exits to make coffee).

EILEEN *How are you, Margaret. Best wishes from everyone of course.*

MARGARET *The days are long and the nights even longer. But I've had a good deal of help, especially in hospital.*

EILEEN *You know we didn't want to trouble you. We certainly didn't want to ask you a lot of questions.*

MARGARET *You may not have been asking me questions, but I've had to ask myself some. You know the most awful moment? It wasn't taking the overdose. You sort of reconcile yourself to that. The most awful moment is when you wake up and a nurse is offering you a cup of tea. You have to face up to everything all over again, and added to that, what you have tried to do and failed. That's when you really do hit the bottom... and weep.*

(Joan returns)

JOAN *Mercifully some help was at hand.*

EILEEN *Thanks.*

MARGARET *Yes. There was a most wonderful young Indian doctor. A psychiatrist. I was so grateful to him. He listened. which was the most important thing to me at the time. He just listened while I talked, and I needed to. It helped. Then he started talking. He introduced me to Ayerveda. He said its origins went back 5000 years. He talked about the three doshas that everyone has. The essence was finding balance. Part of this was to find your true self, accept it, be comfortable with it, even with all of its imperfections. I could only find peace within myself if I could do this. And part of this had to be sharing the truth with you, making my peace with you and with the school.*

EILEEN *Are you sure you want to do this.*

MARGARET *Yes, I am. This cleansing is not just a part of an Indian tradition. Roman Catholics achieve the same at the confessional with their priest. Jews have their own way of atoning. Remember Ben Cohen. He'd been in a car smash and had multiple injuries. In and out of hospital for years. We were able to help him with his education getting medical treatment and physio between hospital visits. Anyway, his dad explained how Jews offloaded their sins. You know their Day of Atonement. That's what we all do. Muslims turn to Allah. We forgive us our trespasses on a daily basis, don't we? Ben's dad summed it up. He said that every housewife knows - and every house husband too - if you Hoover your home on a Monday that's no good reason why you don't have to Hoover it all over again the following Monday.*

FRANK *Some people have got a hell of lot of Hoovering to do. How do the godless manage their guilt without a sin bin?*

MARGARET *Bury it in their subconscious, take Prozac or find a good therapist, like my wonderful Indian doctor. Everyone's got a sin bin, Frank. We've all got to find our own way to manage guilt. We have to learn to live with it, and we have to find a way to forgive it within ourselves. Anyway, what I have to say to you is that I let the school down. They leant on me to tell parents the school had to close. After the last time they thought it would come better from me than from them. They wanted me to drop the bomb on my own school, on everything I've tried to build. And you know the result.*

EILEEN *You really don't need to say any more. We guessed as much. We've all been leant upon here. Yes, leant upon one way or another. I'll tell you something, I have always seen a big difference between hot anger and cold anger. Hot anger flares up, and then dies away, leaving just a trail of ash. Cold anger lingers. You take it to bed with you at night, and you get up with it the following morning. It doesn't just die away.*

JOAN *And that's how you feel?*

EILEEN *Yes I certainly do. It's a great school we have to wave goodbye to.*

FRANK *You're dead right.. I feel exactly the same.   Margaret, I'm so sorry.*

JOAN *I knew, of course. Margaret told me, before it all happened. She said she felt like a little lump of plasticine in the hands of the LEA.*

FRANK *But you didn't want to say.*

JOAN *I couldn't say,, could I? And anyway, I am still not sure what we can now achieve by starting up the fight all over again.. I really can't see it helping the school and the kids. I think that NHS bod, John…*

EILEEN *Lavers?*

JOAN *Yes, John Lavers was probably right. We should draw a line. All I really want to do is to teach. Can't we get back to that simple idea? I will let you into a secret, when I was at school my first love was politics and sociology. The trouble is that these subjects make me angry, and you can't teach in a permanent state of anger, hot or cold. It's not good for you and it is certainly not good for the kids.*

FRANK *You made the right decision? But why English?*

JOAN *Three reasons. First of all I love it. Secondly, I think that every generation has a responsibility to pass on its heritage to the next. That's what teaching is about. Finally, I think we all take our own heritage for granted. We shouldn't. Different countries are chosen to give different things to the world. Greece - democracy and drama, Rome - law and Latin. That was an enormous gift to many Western countries by the Roman Empire, although generations of pupils probably didn't think so . And probably the Romans didn't expect it Italy - sublime Painting, France?*

FRANK *Bloody-mindedness.*

JOAN *No gastronomy, go to the Dordogne. Germany?*

FRANK *Sauerkraut then.*

JOAN *I don't think you're taking me seriously Frank.*

FRANK *Sorry, just a bit of fun.*

JOAN *I'm afraid that national characteristics sometimes aren't funny. For Germany let's say great music.*

JOAN *Anyway we've given over half the world English. We should be a bit more boastful about that. What a huge and totally undervalued legacy of our Empire. It'll last. It enables millions of people to talk to each other.*

FRANK *The Americans haven't done it any favours though, have they?*

JOAN *And texting hasn't helped. But there's been some great American literature, Frank. English is a real treasure house on both sides of the Atlantic. Have you heard of Emily Dickinson?*

FRANK *I'm afraid I haven't.*

JOAN *You've heard of Arthur Miller and Tennessee Williams?*

FRANK *Yes, of course I have.*

JOAN *On our side of the Atlantic, think of William Shakespeare. Think of the great tragedies, Lear, Hamlet, Macbeth, and Othello. Think of our great poets, Wordsworth and Milton and Rupert Brooke, and the writers Charles Dickens, Lewis Carroll and Trollope.... Politics and sociology are not all that far away from them anyway. The human story ... the joy and the pain, the fun and the frolic ... it's all there. The light and shade of human behaviour. The endless fascination of mischief and moment. I can very easily keep my early interest going with our wonderful English language, and without any aggro or torment. That's what I want to give to our kids. And it's for life, not just for exams.*

EILEEN *More strength to you. Look, I don't want any teacher to martyr themselves. It's not worth it. You are all much too valuable. I think we are going to have to accept the inevitable if they carry parents with them. Joan, you just keep teaching. And Margaret, don't feel the need to share your thoughts with anyone else. You've got a career to start up again. Don't lose sight of that, for heaven's sake.*

FRANK   *What was that lovely piece of music you were playing as I arrived?*

MARGARET *It's called "Consolations." Emma sent it to me with her best wishes, and from the kids in her class too. I really appreciated that.*

EILEEN *Play it again.*
(Margaret puts on the CD)

Scene 4

Meeting with parents

In the School Hall, the stage is the platform.

(David Harding, the Director of Education, Gerry Thompson and Ron Smithson are sitting on a platform, David Harding in the chair. Parents and staff have their backs to the audience, acting as its front row. The theatre audience are the parents)

DAVID *Thank you all for coming tonight. I think you probably know why I've asked you to come. I know you're all worried about the future for your kids. I do want to give you my personal assurance you that we do want to do what is best for them. That's what my job is about, nothing else. I've asked your acting head to put you in the picture. Before he does so, there are a couple of things I want to say.…..*

We were all so sorry to hear about Margaret Williamson, your Head teacher. The news I have is that she is very much better. I'm sure you would want to send a message to her tonight wishing her a speedy recovery. Yes?

Secondly, you all know that your wonderful music teacher is leaving you. I'm sure you will all want to congratulate her on her new appointment as regional adviser for music. Do congratulate her and show your appreciation for all she's done for the kids. Your great band will certainly miss her. I've asked your Para Olympian Philippa to make a small presentation.

(Audience encouraged to applaud)

The other thing I must do on behalf of the authority is to thank the Governors for the work they do. I know it's not been easy. They are the greatest resource for voluntary work in the country. There is more than 1 million of them. I don't know where we would be without them.

(Audience encouraged to applaud)

Now I've brought along with me tonight Gerry Thompson, who is in charge of Inclusion. And we'll do our best to answer all your questions. But first I've asked your acting Head, Don Smithson, to say a few words. Before I call on him I would like to thank him for stepping into the breach after Margaret's er... became ill. He's always been a great admirer of this school. Don.

DON *Thank you David. I know you haven't been feeling too well this past week. We appreciate it that you have come this evening, despite that.*

DAVID *I didn't want to miss tonight, Don. I really didn't.*

DON *As David said, I've long been a great admirer of this school. I've a lot of time for the teachers and the carers here. They give so much of themselves to your children. They're a great bunch, and a great team. That's a part of their strength. It's a privilege for me to work with them now. So please don't think I don't understand your feelings when you hear on the grapevine that the LEA still wants to close this school.*

I'll tell you something else. Three years ago you campaigned to keep this school open. I was with you. I was. I for one wasn't surprised when the Minister turned down the proposal to close you down. At that time he was dead right to do so.

But the world has moved on since then. The LEA has responded to your criticism that mainstream schools were not ready to take your children. The staff are now better trained, and more and more parents are pushing to get their kids with special needs into mainstream schools.

Next year there are going to be twenty three fewer children in this school than last year, and the year after fewer still. This has a direct effect on the money the governors can spend. In round figures they're losing nearly two hundred thousand pounds. That has just got to mean job losses. Someone like Emma leaves with a promotion, and the governors can't afford to replace her. Or there are voluntary redundancies or, worse still, compulsory ones.

Now, I said that one of the great strengths of this school was the team. I am sure those who remain will do their level best, but it can't be the same. As your Head I do worry about being able to deliver the national curriculum.

That's why I think you have to listen to what the Director says this evening. That's really all I want to say, David, at this stage. Thank you.

DAVID *Thanks, Don. I don't want to talk about the past. I want to say something about the future. What I want to tell you about is good news and sad news. I say sad news, not bad news.*

The good news first. As you know education is the very first priority for the Council and the Government, and lots of businesses are investing large sums of new money in it. We are all determined to drive up standards in an Inclusive environment where more and more children with special needs can go to mainstream schools. We have a brand new Academy coming here in the next couple of years, and we are investing in all our other schools as well.

Don has told you that this school now has difficulty paying its way. You've contributed to keep it alive. And we have done our best as well. The sad news - and it really isn't bad news - is that good housekeeping requires us to recommend to the School Organisation Committee that the school closes next year.

(Groans from the audience ..*Shame*)

Yes, it is a shame. But times change and we must move on. I do want some of your kids admitted to this new Academy. It will be great for them, a really great opportunity. It will be good for the Academy too. . It's what Inclusion is all about, and I would like some of your teachers to have an opportunity to teach in that school. That too will be a good thing both ways. You were right to fight to keep this school open, but there's a time and a place, and if you were to try to do it again and delay things, some people will certainly lose out. This is not a threat. It's just the way things will happen. I am sure you can see that.

The one thing I want to assure you is that we have a great team, and we are totally committed to make the new world better than the old. This is a time of opportunity for everyone, and if you come with us in this exciting project your children will be in good hands, the best school possible for each of them.

Head teacher leads polite applause from the audience

We'll now take your questions. Who'd like to be first?

JUDY *My son Harry came here from mainstream school. He's got brittle bones. He kept being bullied in his last school and I was for ever taking him to the fracture clinic. At this school there have been no more fractures and no more bullying. Why should I think you are going to look after him better next time?*

DAVID *Gerry would you answer that?*

GERRY *We don't want to get involved with individual problems tonight. Just come and see me afterwards and we'll find a solution. I'm sure there'll be one.*

JOAN *What's going to happen to our staff?*

DAVID *I'm glad you asked that question. They'll get jobs in mainstream schools. Their expertise in special needs will be absolutely invaluable there.*

JILLY *You said that we had fewer kids here because parents didn't want to send their children here. I know two parents in the clinic who were told that you were closing the school.*

DAVID *I'm sure that's not right. We told them that the future was uncertain. We had to tell them that to be fair.*

ANWAR *Are you trying to get rid of Statements?*

DAVID *They are more trouble than they are worth.*

ANWAR *For you maybe, but not for us.*

DAVID *We do have to meet the needs of your children whatever a piece of paper says or doesn't say.*

ANWAR *But we lose our right to a special school for our kids. What about parental choice, hey? What about our choice? Where's that gone?*

QUESTIONER A (In the first row of the real audience) *I had a great problem getting my Stephen into this school. Had to take it through a* tribunal. Much good are your new ideas going to do for Stephen. I think you've tried to starve this school of pupils.

DAVID *Gerry, would you answer that?*

GERRY *We're back to individual cases again. They're all different, and some are difficult to decide. Yours was probably one of them.*

QUESTIONER B (In the first row of the audience) *Some kids will do well in mainstream. What about the rest? Mine has speech problems. She really suffered in mainstream schools before she came here.*

DAVID *You really have got to trust us to work that out at the time. There are still going to be some special schools, you know. We'll do our level best to respect parental preference.*

QUESTIONER B *Are the staff going to have the same amount of time as they give here. Will there be a school nurse all the time? Will there be physio all the time? Will supply teachers know these kids? or are you going to give all the work to classroom assistants?*

DAVID *I make that five questions. Gerry.*

GERRY *That's my responsibility to sort.*

QUESTIONER B *Is that an answer to any of them? Look can we have a vote.*

DON *Can I say something here? This is not that sort of meeting. There are clearly lots of different views this evening. There has been what is called a candid exchange of views. The LEA has to look at the broader picture. They've now got a much clearer view of this bit of it.*

(David leans over to Don and whispers in his ear)

DON *I said that the Director came from his sick bed to be here. He's trying to shake off a bout of flu. He would like to get back to his bed. Can we round off this meeting. Can we thank David and Gerry for coming here tonight? Yes.*

(Don leads polite applause)

I promise you that I'll do my best to see things work out well. And I'm sure that Margaret Williamson, if she was here tonight, would echo that.

Thank you all for coming.

DAVID (walking out with Don) *Thanks for everything, Don. I think they've bought it.*

(David then collapses.)

DON (To the audience) *Is there a doctor here?* (Someone comes forward from the auditorium) *Oh dear, the Director is not very well I'm glad we stopped when we did.*

Scene 5

One month later

Eileen Winterton at her telephone at home and David Harding at his office desk.

EILEEN *Could you put me through to David Harding?*

DAVID *Harding*

EILEEN *Eileen Winterton speaking. I hope you are feeling better.*

DAVID *Yes, I'm pleased to say I am. What can I do for you?*

EILEEN *Have you a moment?*

DAVID *Yes.*

EILEEN *Could we meet?*

DAVID *Have a word with my secretary. She'll fix a time.*

EILEEN *Actually, I meant informally, off the record, possibly over a lunch.*

DAVID *I can never speak entirely off the record, Eileen.*

EILEEN *Well, at least I can say I won't quote anything you say. And please don't quote anything I say.*

DAVID *Okay, I can wear that. What's on your mind?*

EILEEN *The headship and one or two other things.*

DAVID *Have you seen Margaret?*

EILEEN *Yes, I saw her last week.*

DAVID *How is she?*

EILEEN *Better than I thought she'd be.*

DAVID *Okay, maybe we should meet up, and you can debrief me. It'll help. I'd like to know what she said to you. When do you suggest?*

EILEEN *When are you free?*

DAVID *I'll just check my diary.…. How about Tuesday of next week?*

EILEEN *Tuesday's fine by me. How about the Garden Cafe at 1pm?*

DAVID *I've a meeting at 2.30 that afternoon. Should be fine.*

EILEEN *Bring your dancing shoes.*

DAVID *What have you in mind? A Quickstep?*

EILEEN *No, a Foxtrot.*

DAVID *I am definitely not bringing my dancing shoes. See you week Tuesday.* (Puts the phone down) *I wonder what on earth Margaret's been telling her. Soon find out.*

Scene 6

In the Garden Cafe

Eileen Winterton is sitting at a small table. David enters.

DAVID *Hello, I'm sorry I'm late.*

EILEEN *Good to see you. So pleased you could make it.*

DAVID *You do look well. Have you been travelling again?*

EILEEN *Yes, just back from Central America and Panama.*

DAVID *Did you go through the Canal?*

EILEEN *Yes, we did. It was an amazing thing. We heard how it was built. You really see America at its biggest and best.*

DAVID *I think they did bend a few rules as they went along.*

EILEEN *Are you trying to tell me something?*

DAVID *I really wasn't trying to. Believe me. But if you want, raison d'etat when they took over the place, if my memory serves me.*

EILEEN *You mean the State's always entitled to put the boot in.*

DAVID *No, expediency over morality perhaps. But that's the way of it. When was it otherwise?*

EILEEN *No Queensbury Rules?*

DAVID *Those rules are strictly for boxing. They don't apply to sumo wrestling!*

(Waitress arrives with menu)

WAITRESS *Do you want to order now, or do you need more time?*

DAVID *Eileen?*

EILEEN *I'll order now. Baked beans on toast and a pot of tea. English Breakfast, please.*

DAVID *Me, too. A ploughman's and a bottle of sparkling water, with lemon and ice. Many thanks.*

(Waitress leaves)

DAVID *You know I really am not in the rule-breaking business. But I am trying to move things on. The world just doesn't stand still, however much you would like it to. Anyway, tell me. You've seen Margaret. How is she?*

EILEEN *Yes, saw her couple of weeks ago. She's still a bit fragile, but she seems to have shed a load.*

DAVID *What do you mean?*

EILEEN *She said she had had a very good Indian doctor who'd helped her.*

DAVID *Tell me, do you think it was a cry for help, or something else? Did you ask her what happened?*

EILEEN *Oh god no. I wanted to talk about just anything else. I really don't know the answer to your question. I wouldn't even like to hazard a guess. Either way she must have been pretty low. Do you ever think how low kids must get when they are bullied and they try to take their own lives?*

DAVID *I do. Thank God that's never happened on my patch.*

EILEEN *You are very lucky. Childline says that 1,500 suicidal kids call them up every year. I am sure that this never happened when I was at school. Not on this scale.*

DAVID *I keep telling you. The world is a different place these days. You have to deal with it as it is, not as you'd like it to be. Would that it were.*

EILEEN *You've helped to create it. Oh never mind. Back to the here and now then. I do want to know where we go from here in relation to Margaret's job.*

DAVID *I can't give you an answer. We obviously do want to do our very best to help. She's a fine headteacher.*

EILEEN *If the school closes?*

DAVID *When the school closes.*

EILEEN *Okay, when the school closes. Is that absolutely certain?*

DAVID *You must realise that half a school is not better than none, and if more than half the school goes to mainstream, that's the end of it.*

EILEEN *Are you really sure they are ready for it? And our kids aren't going to get bullied there?*

DAVID *Is that your hidden agenda for our lunch?*

EILEEN *No, but I had to raise it. I also wanted to check out Margaret's situation. I do need to know. I feel somehow responsible.*

DAVID *Well, I really can't tell you. We'll have to get medical reports, and then we'll work away from that. If we can recommend her for a new job we'll certainly do so. More than that I can't say, now can I? A lot depends on how she is. I feel responsible too, you know. We put our Heads under a lot of pressure these days. It's not surprising they're in such short supply.*

EILEEN *If she can come back to her old job, if she's well enough, it'll be that much easier for her to move on when the time comes. You really do owe her that, you know.*

DAVID *I think I know where you're coming from. Off the record, yes, you won't quote me? We will do our very best for her.*

EILEEN *I hope you realise that a lot of parents are still upset. I am too you know. A lot of things happened that shouldn't have happened. I still think that you starved us of pupils.*

DAVID *I know what you are saying. We'll just have to differ on that. But things now are as they are. We are going to take a proposal to close the school to the School Organisation Committee. I don't think they will reject it. Please don't fight it. Don't spit at Heaven. It won't help anything. It won't help the kids, it won't help the staff, and I don't think it will actually help Margaret. She's bound to hear about it.*

EILEEN *She's going to be upset whatever she hears, isn't she?*

DAVID *Look lots of things happen today that can be very upsetting. You've just got to keep your eye on the big picture. And so must she. In every garden you can turn over a stone, and you'll find some little grub underneath.*

EILEEN *It's the overgrowing weeds I'm worried about.*

DAVID *You throw weed killer around, and there's no knowing what else you'll kill. I know my garden doesn't meet your organic standards, but I do try to tend the plants. with as much fertiliser as I am given. I'll do my best with Margaret. Trust me.*

(Waitress arrives with food)

DAVID *Look let's enjoy our lunch, and without indigestion afterwards. A ploughman's lunch without a pint of ale is like Christmas without Santa. Tell me about Panama.*

EILEEN *Before we eat I must tell you what I'm going to do.*

DAVID *If you must.*

EILEEN *I am going to argue against anyone suggesting that the school mounts another campaign. I agree with you. That would be awful all round.*

DAVID *I'm very glad about that.*

EILEEN *But I am going to urge the governors to write to your Committee asking them to assure themselves that you can meet the needs of our kids - all of them, after the school closes.*

DAVID *I can't argue with that. In fact, it will probably help me to see that that happens.*

EILEEN *I do hope so. These kids need time and they need their own space too. And they mustn't be bullied. They just mustn't. It will damage some for life if they are.*

DAVID *I know.*

EILEEN *Does Gerry know?*

DAVID *He has a lot to learn, a lot.*

EILEEN *And they need to be stretched, not stressed, to grow and not to be diminished, and to be made to feel whole.*

DAVID *I know that too. Don't think I don't realise. It's just that I'm expected to deliver outcomes as well. It's not easy.*

EILEEN *Outcomes, I do hate that word. I'd ban it altogether. It's so impersonal. Why don't you use the good old English word 'objective'? The word "outcomes" gives jargon a bad name. You have to focus on meeting individual needs if you want to get anywhere at all, and there's no quick fix either.*

DAVID *You and I are really not all that far apart. Look, let's eat. Salt?*

EILEEN *Yes please.*

DAVID *Pepper, too.*

EILEEN *No thank, not today.*

Scene 7

A year later

The scene is outside the School. A bulldozer is slowly demolishing the building. Staff, parents and children watch. Joan Errington and Margaret Williamson have come in together. They are followed by Emma Kirk and the Fawzis and Eileen Winterton.

JOAN *Scurvy politicians seem to see the things thou dost not - King Lear.*

EMMA *Forgive them, for they know not what they do - Jesus Christ.*

EILEEN *I am a bit surprised to see you here.*

EMMA *I owed it to my memories. It's so sad.*

JOAN *Yes, so very sad*

MARGARET *I just felt I had to come. I still wonder whether I could have done anything to prevent this.*

EMMA *Oh for heaven's sake, now don't you say that. This was always going to happen. We all did our best for the kids one way or another. Anyway, how are you keeping?*

MARGARET *Good days and bad, but more good than bad, and the medics said I could get back to work. I feel much more like it now.*

EILEEN *We all hope so too. You are a wonderful Head. The kids love you. And you really stretch them.*

MARGARET *They stretched themselves. I'm applying for a job in the new Academy. I hope that the medics say I am fit enough for that. The LEA thinks I have a good chance to get it, especially with my experience of special needs, and they are a bit short of Head teachers these days.*

EILEEN *You carry all our good wishes. You know that.*

MARGARET *I do and I am grateful for them.*

EILEEN *Hopefully some of our kids will get into the Academy.*

MARGARET *They better had.*

EILEEN *You hope to go there too Joan?*

JOAN *If they'll have me. It's either that or Grovewood Comp.*

MARGARET *That's my alternative too. It does need to be one of them.*

(Johnny, Philippa, Terry and Tracy arrive together)

TRACY *It's a crime*

PHILIPPA *It's a waste.*

JOHNNY *I think it's obscene.*

TERRY *They're all shit.*

MARGARET *Terry, you shouldn't use that word in polite company.*

TERRY *Very sorry miss. It's those new pills I am taking. They don't always work.*

ANWAR *I hate them. Kids have just one chance, and they spoil it for them with their big ideas. And I hate them for something else. They try to make us feel guilty doin' the best for our kids, givin' good schools like this a bad name as a reason for pulling them down. I hate them.*

EMMA *They don't understand. Schools like this have the gift of healing, and they engage the spirit. That's what's so good about them. They just don't understand.*

JUDITH *I really do wish someone would expose the lousy, stinking, hypocritical charade of those who put it about that they care. They say the rights of you kids are paramount. Words. Empty words.. Holy Jesus, you just try to assert those rights today in a tribunal. It's difficult enough as it is.*

ANWAR *And not cheap.*

JUDITH *No, not if you have to get a medical report. And now they're trying to get rid of Statements altogether. Then you'll have no rights at all. They'll try to make out it's in our interests, when it's only in theirs. You know, all they do is play games with people's lives - you kids are just little pawns in a gigantic game of chess.*

MARGARET *Sacrificial pawns, Judith. And for everyone else it's "Snakes and Ladders", with more snakes than ladders.*

EILEEN *In Enron there was another name for it. They called it "rank or yank". You were "ranked" if you played ball with them, "yanked", sacked, if you didn't. Well, no-one blew the whistle, and people lost billions of dollars and their jobs..*

ANWAR *And they play "charades" when it comes to consultation with us parents - they don't really consult - they just want to make it look as though they do.*

EILEEN *And they play "pass the parcel" with our complaints - you know pass the buck. Nobody's accountable for anything these days. That's the real trouble.*

JUDITH *And they play "spinning tops" instead, when they've nothing better to do. They're awful.*

HARRY *What about all those prayers to God, Miss? They don't seem to work..*

EMMA *We are not given to understand everything, Harry. At times her ways are very inscrutable.*

HARRY *What does "'inscrutable" mean?*

EMMA *Well, in my book She's a woman. Sometimes you just don't know whether She's coming or going. Women are like that. They're wired differently. Same power source as men, but different. You'll find out when you're a little older.*

HARRY *So are you still going to sing her praises on Sunday?*

EMMA *Sure I am. She knows how I feel. It's just She's got some catching up to do.*

JOAN *Emma dear, please, 'There is light enough for those who wish to see and darkness enough for those of the opposite disposition.' Blaise Pascal over three hundred years ago. You really don't have to bring God into it.*

EMMA *I do bring God into it. I just fear for her temper these days. One way or another - I think we're really provokin' her. She's capable of quite a tantrum when she's provoked. We'd better be a bit more careful with ourselves, and stop provokin' her.*

JOAN *Well I won't disagree with you there…, God or no God.*

TRACY *Come back in a year and I bet there'll be some lovely houses here.*

HARRY *I bag the house with our swimming pool.*

MARGARET *Rubble, just rubble. Such a pity.*

EMMA *Come on you guys, join me.* (Everyone singing) **"***You are my sunshine, my only sunshine; you* **made** *me happy, when skies* **were** *grey.*

ALL *You'll never know dear, how much I loved you…please don't take my sunshine away.***"**

Bulldozer continues its demolition, and sounds continue for a full minute. Time for quiet contemplation.[35]

Notes and Quotes

1 An OFSTED Report on a Special School 1996

"A good school with many outstanding features... pupils in the school are highly motivated, eager to learn and responsive to the high expectations of their teachers.... the school's ethos is very positive. Teamwork is a strong feature of the school and all staff work closely with a common sense of purpose.... Pupils' moral, social and cultural development is particularly effective ... and pupils develop a strong sense of right and wrong. Social development of pupils is well promoted. The school provides pupils with a range of opportunities within the curriculum and, through an extensive programme of links, to take an active role in a variety of social settings to prepare them for life after school. Pupils' good behaviour is an outstanding feature. When appropriate, pupils assist each other in work and leisure. Relationships with staff are very good."

2 The Case for Inclusion
The Salamanca Statement

More than 300 participants representing 92 governments and 25 international organisations met in Salamanca, Spain in June 1994 to further the aim of *'Education for All'*. This was to consider what basic policy changes were needed to promote inclusive education so that *"schools could serve all children, particularly those with special educational needs."*

I hope that setting it out here will not switch you off. You need to read it to see the ideological content of the Inclusion policy. It is copied directly from http://www.inclusion.com on the Internet.

THE SALAMANCA STATEMENT: NETWORK for ACTION on SPECIAL NEEDS EDUCATION Adopted by the World Conference on Special Needs Education: Access and Quality Salamanca, Spain, 7-10 June 1994

Organised by the Government of Spain and UNESCO, the Conference adopted the Salamanca Statement on Principles, Policy and Practice in Special Needs Education and a Framework for Action.

These two documents are important tools for efforts to make sure schools work better and to fulfil the principle of Education for All. They are printed in a single publication published by UNESCO. Get hold of a copy from the UNESCO office in your country or from the address at the bottom of this page. When you are familiar with its contents, use the two documents to lobby your government for improvements in the education of disabled children and for inclusive education policies.

The Salamanca Statement says that:
- ☐ every child has a basic right to education
- ☐ every child has unique characteristics, interests, abilities and learning needs
- ☐ education services should take into account these diverse characteristics and needs
- ☐ those with special educational needs must have access to regular schools
- ☐ regular schools with an inclusive ethos are the most effective way to combat discriminatory attitudes, create welcoming and inclusive communities and achieve education for all
- ☐ such schools provide effective education to the majority of children and improve efficiency with cost- effectiveness.

The **Salamanca Statement** asks governments to:
- ☐ give the highest priority to making education systems inclusive
- ☐ adopt the principle of inclusive education as a matter of law or policy
- ☐ develop demonstration projects
- ☐ encourage exchanges with countries which have experience of inclusion

- ☐ set up ways to plan, monitor and evaluate educational provision for children and adults
  - • encourage and make easy the participation of parents and organisations of disabled people
  - • invest in early identification and intervention strategies
  - • invest in the vocational aspects of inclusive education
  - • make sure there are adequate teacher education programmes

Phil Wills MP, former Lib Dem spokesman for Education, said in the Commons on 20 March 2001: "Working in Chapeltown in the late 1960's convinced me that unless we could educate the whole community together - wherever they came from and whatever their needs and disabilities - frankly we would breed dysfunctional communities. It is a point of principle to me and my colleagues that inclusive education goes to the heart of the education system."

http://inclusion.uwe.ac.uk/csie provides comprehensive information.

3 A change of policy?
Extracts from House of Commons Education and Skills Committee - Third Report March 2007
A confused message

65. It is widely presumed that the Government has a policy of inclusion or an inclusion agenda. Indeed, Baroness Warnock in her recent article—which many described as a u-turn in her position on inclusion—concluded that "possibly the most disastrous legacy of the 1978 report, was the concept of inclusion." She argued in the article that inclusion could be taken "too far" and that this was resulting in the closure of special schools to the detriment of children with SEN.

66. The Government has, in written and oral evidence to this Committee, repeatedly stated that "it is not Government policy to close special schools" and that "Government plays no role in relation to local authority [...] decisions to close schools."

77. The most radical u-turn was demonstrated by Lord Adonis in his evidence to the Committee. The Minister described the Government as being "content" if, as a result of Local Authority decisions, the current "roughly static position in respect of special schools" continues.

78. Lord Adonis specifically said that the Government:
"do not have a view about a set proportion of pupils who should be in special schools."

79. This directly contradicts the stated aim in the 2004 SEN Strategy that "the proportion of children educated in special schools should fall over time". The Minister's words demonstrate a significant change in policy direction.

5 July 2007 Schools Minister Andrew Adonis has announced a further £23 million to expand the number of SEN specialist schools over the next three years. This will mean around 150 schools becoming specialist SEN schools.

4 "Human Rights" - Extract from Essay 8 - Essays in Jurisprudence and Philosophy by H.L.A. Hart

Page 196   There is however no doubt that the conception of basic human rights has deeply affected the style of diplomacy, the morality, and the political ideology of our time, even though thousands of innocent persons still imprisoned or oppressed have not yet felt its benefits. The doctrine of human rights has at least temporarily replaced the doctrine of maximizing utilitarianism as the prime philosophical inspiration of political and social reform. It remains to be seen whether it will have such success as utilitarianism once had in changing the practices of governments for human good.

5 Pupil perceptions

Mainstream pupils, few of whom had special school experiences, had mostly positive views about special schools. Mainly negative views were held by about one in five, with slightly more, about a quarter, holding mixed views This was different for special school pupils, where the majority had had mainstream school experiences. For them, only about one in six had mainly positive views of mainstream schools, whereas about half had mixed views, with about a third having mainly negative views. This difference could be due to special school pupils' 'bad' experiences in the mainstream, and mainstream pupils' lack of experience of special schools.

Page 163 *Moderate Learning Difficulties and the Future of Inclusion*, Braham Norwich and Narcie Kelly.

6 The Bullying of Children with Learning Disabilities - ENABLE Scotland 2007

Our work with our Young People's Self Advocacy Groups has revealed that bullying is also an important issue for children and young people with learning disabilities. We joined forces with Mencap to undertake UK wide research to find out the scale and nature of the problem and most importantly to tell us more about how to stop it.

We knew that bullying of children with learning disabilities existed. We knew that it is widespread and has a significant effect on children's lives. However, we were shocked by the results that the survey revealed. We could not have predicted the scale of the problem.

- The sheer numbers of children who were bullied

- The persistence of bullying throughout childhood

- The failure of adults to stop bullying when it is reported

- The range of places where bullying takes place

- The effects bullying has on the emotional state of children

- The social exclusion faced by children who are afraid to go out

Bullying is not just a part of growing up. ENABLE Scotland believes that no child should have to put up with bullying and that we all have a responsibility to speak up to ensure that this stops.

Report Summary
Headline Results

- 93% of children with learning disabilities have been bullied

- 46% of children with learning disabilities have been physically assaulted

- Half have been bullied persistently for more than two years

- Bullying is not just a school issue

- 40% are too scared to go to places where they have been bullied

7 Extracts from Education Policy Partnership, December 2003 Review - *The impact of paid adult support on the participation and learning of pupils in mainstream schools*

A recent government consultation paper on the role of school support staff DfES, 2002 indicated that there were over 100,000 working in schools - an increase of over 50 percent since 1997.

- Paid adult support staff can sometimes be seen as stigmatising the pupils they support. Paid adult support staff can sometimes thwart inclusion by working in relative isolation with the pupils they are supporting and by not helping their pupils, other pupils in the class and the classroom teacher to interact with each other.

- Paid adult support shows no consistent or clear overall effect on class attainment scores. Paid adult support may have an impact on individual but not class test scores.

- Most significantly, there is evidence from several studies of a tension between paid adult support behaviour that contributes to short-term changes in pupils, and those which are associated with the longer-term developments of pupils as learners. Paid adult support strategies associated with on-task behaviour in the short term do not necessarily help pupils to construct their own identity as learners, and some studies in this cluster suggest that in such strategies can actively hinder this process.

- Paid adult support staff can positively affect on-task behaviour of students through their close proximity. Continuous close proximity of paid adult support can have unintended, negative effects on longer-term aspects of pupil participation and teacher engagement. Less engaged teachers can be associated with the isolation of both students with disabilities and their support staff, insular relationships between paid adult support staff and students, and stigmatisation of pupils who come to reject the close proximity of paid adult support.

- Given current interest in involving users in planning, carrying out and evaluating research, it is surprising that so few studies actually focus on the pupils' views.

8 Extracts from *Costs and Outcomes for Pupils with Moderate Learning Difficulties in Special and Mainstream Schools 1999*

p 14 We have some generalized findings on outcomes from our literature survey and these are highly suggestive - but they do not make it possible to evaluate the cost-effectiveness of the schools in our study,..... For many, inclusion is a fundamental human right - not simply one form of SEN provision amongst many, to be evaluated on the balance of advantage it confers on children. It is important to be clear, therefore, that an analysis of costs and outcomes cannot properly be used to determine questions of rights.

P71 The state of our knowledge about outcomes for pupils with MLD is not good, and our understanding of the relationship between costs and outcomes is even worse.

P 107 Appendix 4 LEA Survey

Requests for information = 145 excluding 8 LEAs involved in the research

33 LEAs responded to this request:

- 76% do not have any information/studies

- 15% sent limited information but do not have any significant current studies.

- 9% sent information or undertaking studies.

9 From *Leadership* by Rudolph Giuliani

The New York City school system was never really going to improve until its purpose, its core mission, was made clear. What the system *should* have been about was educating its million children as well as possible. Instead, it existed to provide jobs for the people who worked in it, and to preserve those jobs regardless of performance. That's not to say that there weren't committed professionals at every level within the system. There were, and that's the shame of it. Those with their hearts in the right place were the ones who suffered most.

Until I could get everyone involved to sit together and agree that the system existed to educate children, fixing little bits of it was symbolic at best. Band-Aid solutions can do more harm than good. The system needed a new philosophy. It needed to say we're not a job protection system but a system at its core about children's enrichment. All rewards and risks must flow from the performance of the children. If you took a broken system and repaired just enough so that it could limp along, you lessened the chance that a real and lasting solution could be reached. That's why I resist partial control over a project. The schools should be made into a mayoral agency—like the Administration for Children's Services or the Fire Department— so the city can enact real solutions.

10 The Power Inquiry

This Inquiry was set up by the Joseph Rowntree Trust in 2004 to mark its centenary.

It established a Commission under the chair of Baroness Helena Kennedy QC, to investigate why the decline in popular participation and involvement in formal politics has occurred, to provide concrete and innovative proposals to reverse the trend and to explore how public participation and involvement can be increased and deepened. Its work was based on the primary belief that a healthy democracy requires the active participation of its citizens. It is completely independent of any political party or organisation. It works across the political spectrum and, most importantly, with people who feel that the political parties do not represent them anymore.

The Commission published its final report, *Power to the People*, in February 2006. The report outlined 30 recommendations for change, but most importantly it argues that there is a need for a re-balancing of power between the Executive and Parliament, between Central and Local Government and between the Citizen and the State. www.makeitanissue http.org.uk.

11 Pills and pills!

Mental Health Supplement, in *The Times* 27 November 2007

Perpetual sunshine

"Between 1991 and 2001 antidepressant prescriptions in the UK rose from 9 million to 24 million a year." And they are still rising.

Guardian Unlimited   12 November 2007

Ritalin of no long-term benefit, study finds

Research released today raises questions about the long-term effectiveness of drugs used to treat attention deficit hyperactivity disorder (ADHD).

A team of American scientists conducting the Multimodal Treatment Study of Children with ADHD (MTA) has found that while drugs such as Ritalin and Concerta can work well in the short term, over a three-year period they brought about no demonstrable improvement in children's behaviour. They also found the drugs could stunt growth.

The research, which will be broadcast on the BBC Panorama programme tonight, shows that GPs in the UK prescribed ADHD drugs such as Ritalin and Concerta to around 55,000 children last year – at a cost of £28m to the NHS.

The MTA's warning about ADHD drugs constitutes something of a revised opinion. The scientists, who have been monitoring the treatment of 600 children across the US since the 1990s, concluded in 1999 that, after one year, medication worked better than behavioural therapy for ADHD. This finding influenced medical practice on both sides of the Atlantic and prescription rates in the UK have since tripled.

The report's co-author, Professor William Pelham, of the University of Buffalo, said: "I think we exaggerated the beneficial impact of medication in the first study. We had thought that children medicated longer would have better outcomes. That didn't happen to be the case.

"The children had a substantial decrease in their rate of growth, so they weren't growing as much as other kids in terms of both their height and their weight. And the second was that there were no beneficial effects - none.

"In the short run [medication] will help the child behave better, in the long run it won't. And that information should be made very clear to parents."

Dr Tim Kendall, of the Royal College of Psychiatrists, who is helping prepare new NHS guidelines for the treatment of ADHD, said: "A generous understanding would be to say that doctors have reached the point where they don't know what else to offer.

"I hope we will be able to make recommendations that will give people a comprehensive approach to treatment and that will advise about what teachers might be able to do within the classroom when they're trying to deal with kids who have difficult problems of this kind.

"I think the important thing is we have a comprehensive approach that doesn't focus on just one type of treatment."

The new treatment guidelines will be published next year.

12 David could not tie his shoe-laces

Anthony Storr writes "David, a six-year-old autistic boy, suffered from chronic anxiety and poor visual-motor co-ordination. For nine months, efforts had been made to teach him to tie his shoe-laces without avail. However, it was discovered that his audio motor co-ordination was excellent. He could beat quite complex rhythms on a drum, and was clearly musically gifted. When a student therapist put the process of tying his shoe-laces into a song, David succeeded at the second attempt."

13 *Médecins sans Frontières*

Doctors without borders is an international nongovernmental organisation with humane goal of French origin.

It urgently offers a medical care in cases like the wars, the natural disasters, the epidemics and the famines. MSF offers also longer-term actions at the time of prolonged conflicts or chronic instability, within the framework of the assistance to the refugees or following catastrophes.

It was created December 20 1971 by French doctors who had gone to Biafra after its secession.

MSF received the Nobel Prize of peace in 1999 in reward of its combat in favour of the humane interference.

Extracted from *Wikipedia*

14 Mother Teresa

Mother Teresa (1910 –1997) was a Roman Catholic nun who founded the Missionaries of Charity and won the Nobel Peace Prize in 1979 for her humanitarian work. For over forty years, she ministered to the needs of the poor, sick, orphaned, and dying in Calcutta, India.

As the Missionaries of Charity grew under Mother Teresa's leadership, they expanded their ministry to other countries. By the 1970s she had become internationally famed as a humanitarian and advocate for the poor and helpless, due in part to a documentary, and book, *Something Beautiful for God* by Malcolm Muggeridge.

Following her death she was beatified by Pope John Paul II and given the title Blessed Teresa of Calcutta.

Extracted from Wikipedia

15 Archbishop Desmond Tutu

Desmond Mpilo Tutu born 7 October 1931 is a South African cleric and activist who rose to worldwide fame during the 1980s as an opponent of apartheid. Tutu was elected and ordained the first black South African Anglican Archbishop of Cape Town, South Africa, and primate of the Church of the Province of Southern Africa now the Anglican Church of Southern Africa. He was awarded the Nobel Peace Prize in 1984. He is also a recipient of the Albert Schweitzer Prize for Humanitarianism and was also rewarded with the Magubela prize for liberty in 1986. Desmond Tutu is committed to stopping global AIDS, and has served as the honorary chairman for the Global AIDS Alliance. In February 2007 he was awarded Gandhi Peace Prize by Dr. A.P.J. Abdul Kalam, president of India.

He was generally credited with coining the term Rainbow Nation as a metaphor to describe post-apartheid South Africa after 1994 under ANC rule. The expression has since entered mainstream consciousness to describe South Africa's ethnic diversity.

Extracted from Wikipedia

16 Martin Luther King Jnr.

Rev.Martin Luther King, Jnr. 1929 –1968 was one of the main leaders of the American civil rights movement. He was a political activist and Baptist minister and is regarded as one of America's greatest orators. King's most influential and well-known public address is the "I Have A Dream" speech, delivered on the steps of the Lincoln Memorial in Washington, D.C. in 1963. In 1964, King became the youngest man to be awarded the Nobel Peace Prize for his work as a peacemaker, promoting non-violence and equal treatment for different races. On April 4, 1968, King was assassinated in Memphis, Tennessee.

In 1977, he was posthumously awarded the Presidential Medal of Freedom by Jimmy Carter. In 1986, Martin Luther King Day was established as a United States holiday. In 2004, King was awarded a Congressional Gold Medal.

Extracted from Wikipedia

17 Mahatma Ghandi

Gandhi 1869 –1948 was a major political and spiritual leader of India and the Indian independence movement. He was the pioneer of Satyagraha—the resistance of tyranny through mass civil disobedience, firmly founded upon ahimsa or total non-violence—which was one of the strongest driving philosophies of the Indian independence movement and inspired movements for civil rights and freedom across the world. Gandhi is commonly known in India and across the world as Mahatma Gandhi mahatma – "Great Soul" and as *Bapu bāpu* – "Father". In India, he is officially accorded the honour of Father of the Nation and October 2nd, his birthday, is commemorated each year as Gandhi Jayanti, a national holiday. On 15 June 2007, the United Nations General Assembly unanimously adopted a resolution declaring October 2 to be the "International Day of Non-Violence."

Extracted from Wikipedia

18 His Holiness the 14th Dalai Lama, Tenzin Gyatso

His Holiness the 14th Dalai Lama, Tenzin Gyatso, is both the head of state and the spiritual leader of Tibet. He was born on 6 July 1935, to a farming family, in a small hamlet located in Taktser, Amdo, northeastern Tibet. At the age of two the child, who was named Lhamo Dhondup at that time was recognized as the reincarnation of the 13th Dalai Lama, Thubten Gyatso. The Dalai Lamas are believed to be manifestations of Avalokiteshvara or Chenrezig, the Bodhisattva of Compassion and patron saint of Tibet. Bodhisattvas are enlightened beings who have postponed their own nirvana and chosen to take rebirth in order to serve humanity.

Three Main Commitments in Life

Firstly, on the level of a human being, His Holiness' first commitment is the promotion of human values such as compassion, forgiveness, tolerance, contentment and self-discipline. All human beings are the same. We all want happiness and do not want suffering. Even people who do not believe in religion recognize the importance of these human values in making their life happier. His Holiness refers to these human values as secular ethics. He remains committed to talk about the importance of these human values and share them with everyone he meets.

Secondly, on the level of a religious practitioner, His Holiness' second commitment is the promotion of religious harmony and understanding among the world's major religious traditions. Despite philosophical differences, all major world religions have the same potential to create good human beings. It is therefore important for all religious traditions to respect one another and recognize the value of each other's respective traditions. As far as one truth, one religion is concerned, this is relevant on an individual level. However, for the community at large, several truths, several religions are necessary.

Thirdly, His Holiness is a Tibetan and carries the name of the 'Dalai Lama'. Tibetans place their trust in him. Therefore, his third commitment is to the Tibetan issue. His Holiness has a responsibility to act as the free spokesperson of the Tibetans in their struggle for justice. As far as this third commitment is concerned, it will cease to exist once a mutually beneficial solution is reached between the Tibetans and Chinese.

However, His Holiness will carry on with the first two commitments till his last breath.

*www.**dalailama**.com*

19 The Prophets

*And what does God require of you. But to do justice, to love mercy and to walk humbly with your God. **Micah 6:8**. And now abideth faith, hope, charity, these three; but the greatest of these is charity. **I Corinthians 13:13**. Those who make a display of piety but have not committed their whole lives to compassionate action are like those who perform daily prayers as habit or as convention, without true awe, humility, and longing. Since their religion remains mere pretence, the vessel of their being has not been filled with active kindness by the Source of Love. **Koran 107:1-7***

20 The Seven Laws of Noah

Often referred to as the **Noahide Laws,** these are a list of seven moral imperatives which were given by God to Noah as a binding set of laws for all mankind. They have been recognised in the United States Congress: "Whereas Congress recognizes the historical tradition of ethical values and principles which are the basis of civilized society and upon which our great Nation was founded; whereas these ethical values and principles have been the bedrock of society from the dawn of civilization."

21 The Dignity of Difference by Chief Rabbi, Sir Jonathan Sacks

"So too in the case of religion. The radical transcendence of God in the Hebrew Bible means that the Infinite lies beyond our finite understanding. God communicates in human language, but there are dimensions of the divine that must forever elude us. As Jews we believe that God has made a covenant with a singular people, but that does not exclude the possibility of other peoples, cultures and faiths finding their own relationship with God within the shared frame of the Noahide laws. These laws constitute, as it were, the depth grammar of the human experience of the divine: of what it is to see the world as God's work and humanity as God's image. *God is God of all humanity, but between Babel and the end of days no single faith is the faith of all humanity.* Such a narrative would lead us to respect the search for God in people of other faiths and reconcile the particularity of cultures with the universality of the human condition."

22 The Alexandria Declaration *January 2002*

"In the name of God who is Almighty, Merciful and Compassionate, we, who have gathered as religious leaders from the Muslim, Christian and Jewish communities, pray for true peace in Jerusalem and the Holy Land, and declare our commitment to ending the violence and bloodshed that denies the right of life and dignity.

According to our faith traditions, killing innocent in the name of God is a desecration of His Holy Name, and defames religion in the world. The violence in the Holy Land is an evil which must be opposed by all people of good faith. We seek to live together as neighbours respecting the integrity of each other's historical and religious inheritance. We call upon all to oppose incitement, hatred and misrepresentation of the other.

Delegates:
- His Grace the Archbishop of Canterbury, Dr. George Carey
- His Eminence Sheikh Mohamed Sayed Tantawi, Cairo, Egypt
- Sephardi Chief Rabbi Bakshi-Doron
- Deputy Foreign Minister of Israel, Rabbi Michael Melchior
- Rabbi of Tekoa, Rabbi Menachem Froman

- International Director of Interreligious Affairs, American Jewish Committee, Rabbi David Rosen
- Rabbi of Savyon, Rabbi David Brodman
- Rabbi of Maalot Dafna, Rabbi Yitzak Ralbag
- Chief Justice of the Sharia Courts, Sheikh Taisir Tamimi
- Minister of State for the PA, Sheikh Tal El Sider
- Mufti of the Armed Forces, Sheikh Abdelsalam Abu Schkedem
- Mufti of Bethlehm, Sheikh Mohammed Taweel
- Representative of the Greek Patriarch, Archibishop Aristichos
- Latin Patriarch, His Beatitude Michel Sabbah
- Melkite Archbishop, Archbishop Boutrous Mu'alem
- Representative of the Armenian Patriarch, Archbishop Chinchinian
- Bishop of Jerusalem, The Rt. Rev. Riah Abu El Assal

23 The uncertainties of science

"I have never known in quite a long life to be faced with so many unanswered questions. It is quite extraordinary that young people speak and teach about the evolution of the Universe and the Big Bang, and yet we have no idea what 95 per cent of the matter and energy in the Universe consists of." Sir Bernard Lovell, *The Times* 2 June 2007.

24 *Death of a Nightingale Fund*

All the royalties from this book will be donated in perpetuity to *Death of a Nightingale Fund* within the *Community Foundation serving Tyne & Wear* to the benefit of children with special educational needs. In particular this Fund will make regular contributions to:

- The Rotary Foundation within Rotary International. Rotary is a worldwide organisation of business and professional leaders that provides humanitarian service, encourages high ethical standards in all vocations, and helps build goodwill and peace in the world. Approximately 1.2 million Rotarians belong to more than 32,000 clubs in more than 200 countries and geographical areas.

- The Children's Foundation which raises essential funds for medical and lifestyle research to combat childhood diseases and conditions such as cerebral palsy and autism. It supports NHS service delivery and a number of innovative, community-based projects, designed to improve and protect the health and wellbeing of children and young people. Their partnership programmes help children in North East England but ultimately children everywhere.

- The Jerusalem Foundation promotes a civil society in Jerusalem - free, tolerant, enlightened, advanced and pluralistic in accordance with the spirit of the Founder Teddy Kollek. It sets out to strengthen the social fabric of Jerusalem, as a society open to all opinions, views and creeds. Many projects are aimed at bettering the understanding between all segments of society living in Jerusalem. While the majority of the trustees of the Foundation are Jews, there are also a number of Moslem and Christian trustees.

- Neve Shalom / Wahat al- Salaam: Hebrew and Arabic for *Oasis of Peace* [Isaiah 32:18]. This is a village, jointly established by Jewish and Palestinian Arab citizens of Israel that is engaged in educational work for peace, equality and understanding between the two peoples.

25 Special Needs - Legal Rights in UK

Clause I 3, 2001 SEN Act: *'If a statement is maintained under section 324 for the child, he must be educated in a mainstream school unless that is incompatible with - a the wishes of his parent, or b the provision of efficient education for other children.'* My underlining

Catchpole v Buckingham County Council and another, The *Times* Law Reports on 18 March 1999, Lord Justice Thorpe said *"the local education authority had a duty to ensure that a child with special education needs was placed at a school that was appropriate. It was not enough for the school to be merely adequate."*

Phelps v Hillingdon Borough Council, Anderton v Clwyd County Council, Gower v Bromley London Borough Council and Jarvis v Hampshire Country Council. Times Law Reports, July 28, 2000. The House of Lords ruled that LEAs duty of care required them to *"have to take reasonable care of their health and safety including the monitoring of their needs and performance."*

26 The Notting Hill Carnival

This is an annual event which takes place in Notting Hill, London, England each August, over three days. It is led by members of the Caribbean population, many of whom have lived in the area since the 1950s. The carnival has attracted up to 1.5 million people in the past, putting it among the largest street festivals in Europe.

27 Savile Row

This street occupies a quiet corner of Mayfair in central London and is famous the world over as the home of men's bespoke tailoring.

Many of the greatest, most famous men have patronised the many tailors that occupy this street, men such as Winston Churchill, Lord Nelson, and Napoleon III.

The Row runs parallel to Regent Street between Conduit Street at the northern end and Vigo Street at the southern. Linking roads include Burlington Place, Clifford Street and Burlington Gardens.

28 The man on the Clapham omnibus

This saying is the lawyer's description of the reasonable man, an ordinary sort of guy, sensible but non-specialist — a hypothetical person against whom a defendant's conduct might be judged in English Civil Law. The description was first used by Lord Justice Greer in *Hall v. Brooklands Auto-Racing Club* 1933 1 KB 205

29 The Dome

This was originally built in London for the Millennium celebrations. It is the largest structure of its kind in the world. The circumference of The Dome exceeds 1km, and the floor-space is large enough to park 18,000 London buses! The Jubilee Line on the London Underground was extended to reach it. Financially it was a huge cost to the taxpayer, and as the Dome it was a very large white elephant *we* will never forget. It has, however, come right in the end. It is now O_2, a spectacular entertainment complex. Once it was a showpiece for New Labour's vision of the UK, now it is a showpiece for capitalism, but at the taxpayers' expense. Mercifully it is not a Casino.

30 School Organisation Committees

These committees are independent statutory bodies set up under the provisions of the School Standards and Framework Act 1998.Their principal role is to examine proposals for the closure and/or opening of schools as brought forward by a Local Education Authorities. They comprise: representatives from the Local Authority, elected Councillor Members, and nominees from the Church of England, the Catholic Church, the Learning and Skills Council and from the School Group School Governor representatives from the Primary/Secondary and Special sector schools.

31 The Luddites

They were a social movement of English textile artisans in the early nineteenth century who protested — often by destroying textile machines — against the changes produced by the Industrial Revolution, which they felt threatened their livelihood.

32 Peekskill 4 September 1949

Why did a concert given by Paul Robeson in New York State provoke a riot? He was a singer with a fine bass voice, and the first to bring spirituals to the concert hall. He was a notable actor on stage and in film. But he was much else besides. His father had been a run-a-way slave later becoming a church minister. His mother came from an abolitionist Quaker family. He had won an academic scholarship to Rutgers University, the only black student on campus at the time, and one of three classmates accepted into Phi Beta Kappa. He was a noted sportsman and athlete.

It was, however, as a civil rights activist campaigning against lynching, and as a supporter of the Soviet Union after World War II, that provoked the savage backlash in Peekskill that Labor weekend in 1949. Over fifteen thousand people had attended the concert, and hundreds of them were injured, some seriously, as they tried to make their way home. He was an iconic figure in the fight against racial prejudice. In the Soviet Union he said that he found a country free of racial prejudice, and as he sang in concerts around the world he said that Afro-American spiritual music resonated to Russian folk traditions, and he preached their common humanity. Not everyone agreed with him at the time.

33 Helen Keller

Helen Keller was born in Tuscumbia, Alabama, on June 27, 1880, to parents Captain Arthur H. Keller, a former officer of the Confederate Army, and Kate Adams Keller, cousin of Robert E. Lee. She was not born blind and deaf; it was not until nineteen months of age that she came down with an illness that did not last for a particularly long time, but it left her deaf and blind. At that time her only communication partner was Martha Washington, the 6-year old daughter of the family cook, who was able to create a sign language with Helen, so that by age seven, she had over sixty different signs to communicate with her family

In 1886, her mother Kate Keller was inspired by an account in Charles Dickens' American Notes of the successful education of another deaf blind child, Laura Bridgman, and travelled to a doctor in Baltimore for advice. He put her in touch with local expert Alexander Graham Bell, who was working with deaf children at the time. Bell advised the couple to contact the Perkins Institute for the Blind, the school where Bridgman had been educated, which was then located in South Boston, Boston, Massachusetts. The school delegated teacher and former student, Anne Sullivan, herself visually impaired and then only 20 years old, to become Keller's teacher. It was the beginning of a 49-year-long relationship.

Helen's big breakthrough in communication came one day when she realized that the motions her teacher was making on her palm, while running cool water over her palm from a pump, symbolized the idea of "water;" she then nearly exhausted Sullivan demanding the names of all the other familiar objects in her world including her prized doll.. Anne was able to teach Helen to speak using the Tadoma method touching the lips and throat of others as they speak combined with "fingerspelling" alphabetical characters on the palm of Helen's hand. Later, Keller would also learn to read English, French, German, Greek, and Latin in Braille.

In 1888, Keller attended the Perkins School for the Blind. In 1894, Keller and Sullivan moved to New York City to attend the Wright-Humason School for the Deaf and Horace Mann School for the Deaf. In 1896 they returned to Massachusetts and Helen entered The Cambridge School for Young Ladies before gaining admittance, in 1900, to Radcliffe College, where Standard Oil magnate Henry Huttleton Rogers paid for her education. In 1904 at the age of 24, Keller graduated from Radcliffe magna cum laude, becoming the first deaf and blind person to graduate from a college.

Helen Keller wrote *Light in my Darkness*, which was published in 1960. In the book, she advocates the teachings of the Swedish scientist and philosopher Emanuel Swedenborg. She also wrote an autobiography called *The Story of My Life*, which was published in 1903.. In total, she wrote twelve books and authored numerous articles.

Extracted from Wikipedia

34 Sikhism,

This, the youngest of the world religions, is barely five hundred years old. Its founder, Guru Nanak, was born in 1469. Guru Nanak spread a simple message of "Ek Ong Kar": we are all one, created by the One Creator of all Creation. This was at a time when India was being torn apart by castes, sectarianism, religious factions, and fanaticism. He aligned with no religion, and respected all religions. He expressed the reality that there is one God and many paths, and the Name of God is Truth, "Sat Nam".

The foundation of Sikhism was laid down by Guru Nanak. Guru Nanak infused his own consciousness into a disciple, who then became Guru, subsequently passing the light on to the next, and so on. The word "Guru" is derived from the root words "Gu", which means darkness or ignorance, and "Ru", which means light or knowledge The Guru is the experience of Truth God.

Each one of the ten Gurus represents a divine attribute:

Guru Nanak - Humility
Guru Angad - Obedience
Guru Amar Das — Equality
Guru Ram Das - Service
Guru Arjan - Self-Sacrifice
Guru Hargobind - Justice
Guru Har Rai - Mercy
Guru Harkrishan - Purity
Guru Tegh Bahadur - Tranquillity
Guru Gobind Singh - Royal Courage

This is taken directly from www.sikhnet.com

35 Conclusion - Questions for Quiet Contemplation

The play is about special education needs. Feel free to stop it at this point.

But press on if you care to. As I said at the outset, the play is a tiny snapshot. It also affords a peep-hole to a larger picture. In some ways it is a parable for our times. I am uncomfortable with the dogma of Inclusion. I also sense unease about the future of our world as we live off it, and you may feel it too. All things, after all, have their life cycle. So I have allowed my mind to meditate on these things, and you may care to do the same.

There can always be renewal and refreshment.

People have asked me who I have written this for. The answer obviously is for anyone interested enough to want to read it. But I have had in my mind those who have a care and concern for the rising generation of children, in particular their parents, their teachers and those with specific responsibility for them. I pose questions especially for them - but not just for them - which they might like to think about. I give some short answers knowing full well that there are sometimes very long answers or no easy answers at all.

What I do know, however, is the power of the written and the spoken word. Way back in time it was transmitted from memory, more recently on the printed page, and now on the Internet. It is our greatest resource, and we must all use it.

Here are some questions I invite you to think about.

1. What stands between us and the destruction of things we treasure?

2. Who threatens it?

3. Where does our strength reside?

4. Which is the wiser mantra in education - Equality or Equity?

5. How far does declaring a "Right" provide the protection of "a Right"?

6. How do we reconcile an increasingly controlling society with a participating one?

7. How do we get a more efficient, less wasteful system of Government?

8. How do we get better directed policies from all political parties?

9 How does a multicultural society live at peace with itself?

10 Is this generation properly mindful of the legacy it is bequeathing to the grandchildren of its grandchildren?

My short answers

1. A sense of our common humanity and an appreciation of our diverse needs

2. The common denominator here - all those who abuse their power over people.

The little Hitlers as well as the big Hitlers, and not just politicians. People in all walks of life, religious as well as secular.

3. In life force and in the human spirit. So encourage the young to aspire, to work together, to put a value on self-esteem and to uphold standards of conduct and behaviour.

4. One child's opportunity can be another child's road block. I go for Equity every time.

5. Sometimes, but certainly not always.

6. Structure in that participation ... and make it stick. Lip service is not enough. Those who say that they want to achieve this should say how they plan to do so.

7. Make it fully accountable, with no greater job security than exists in the private sector. Once upon a time someone set standards. Today everyone excuses their absence.

8. Make them sensitive to individual need - not just projecting their own needs on everyone else, and calling them outcomes.

9. With mutual respect, remembering that healthy respect cannot be a one-way street, that love is a bonus, and hatred the enemy.

10. No.

Bibliography

Towards Inclusive Schooling by Mel Ainscow British Journal of Special Education Volume 24 No 1 March 1997

The Role of LEAs in Developing Inclusive Policies and Practices, by Mel Ainscow, Peter Farrell, Dave Tweddle and George Malki,

Families Back Drive for Special Education Overhaul; after Warnock's Climb down. Pressure for Change The Daily Mail, June 10, 2005.

The Next Step for Special Education by Mel Ainscow, British Journal of Special Education Volume 27 No2 June 2000 *SEN and Disability Rights in Education Bill*, Consultation Document published by the DfEE, and the *2001 Act* itself.

Costs and Outcomes for Pupils with Moderate Learning Difficulties in Special and Mainstream Schools, Research Report RR89 published by DfEE December 1998

SEN Code of Practice on the Identification and Assessment of Pupils with Special Educational Needs & SEN Thresholds: Good Practice Guidance ... Consultation Papers published by the DfEE in July 2000

SEN Code of Practice DfES 581/2001, November 2001

Removing Barriers to Achievement - The Government's Strategy for SEN, DfES Publications DfES/0117/2004

The wrong debate by Alan Dyson, *Special* Spring 2000, published by NASEN.

Education Act 1996

Excellence in Schools, Government White Paper published by the Stationery Office July 1997

British Journal of Special Education Volume 26 No 3 September 1999 *Educational Inclusion and Raising Standards* by Michael Farrell, British Journal of Special Education Volume 27 No1 March 2000

The Debate That Never Happened by Charles Gains and Philip Garner *Special* Autumn 2000 Published by NASEN

The Debate Begins by Philip Garner and Charles Gains, *Special* Spring 2001, published by NASEN.

Enabling Inclusion Blue Skies ... Dark Clouds? Contributions by special needs and educational professionals, The Stationery Office 2001

The Prophet by Kahil Gibran, Alfred A. Knopf, 1923 ISBN 0394404289

Leadership by Rudolph W. Giuliani, publisher, Buchet Chastel March 16, 2003

The Lord of the Flies by William Golding, Faber and Faber; New Ed edition, 1997

Hansard Report of the Second Reading of Special Educational Needs and Disability Bill in the House of Lords on 19 December 2000, and of the Grand Committee on 23 January 2001

Hansard Report of the Second Reading of the Special Educational Needs and Disability Bill in the House of Commons on 20 March 2001

Essays in Jurisprudence and Philosophy H.L.A.Hart Oxford University Press, reprinted 2001.

Forward to Ethics of Special Education K R Howe and O.B Miramontes New York by J M Kauffman Teachers College Press 1992

Whitehall's Black Box: Accountability and performance in the senior civil service Institute for Public Policy Research ISBN: 1860302998 August 2006

What does 'Inclusion' Mean for Children with Physical Disabilities, an Occasional Paper by Dr. Ann Llewellyn Special Children February 2001

Helen Keller Quotes http://thinkexist.com/quotes/helen_keller/4.html

The impact of paid adult support on the participation and learning of pupils in mainstream schools EPP December 2003 Review

Meeting Special Educational Needs - A programme of action, ISBN 085522 906 3 published 1998.

Meeting Special Educational Needs: A programme for Action DfEE, 1998

Moderate Learning Difficulties and the Future of Inclusion, Braham Norwich and Narcie Kelly. RoutledgeFalmer 2005 ISBN 0-415-31974-9

1984 by George Orwell, Signet Classics.

Power to the People http://www.parliament.uk/commons/lib/research/notes/snpc-03948.pdf

The Dignity of Difference: How to Avoid the Clash of Civilizations by Chief Rabbi Sir Jonathan Sacks. Publisher: Continuum International Publishing Group; 2 Sub edition July 2003

Music and the Mind by Anthony Storr, Harper Collins Publishers, 1992.

Valuing People - A New Strategy for Learning Disability for the 21st Century Cm5086 published by the Department of Health March 2001

About the Author

For over 17 years a governor of a special school for children with a physical difficulty and an associated learning difficulty, chair of governors for most of that time. A degree in Jurisprudence at Merton College, Oxford. A barrister, but practiced for only three years. Left the Bar to work for the Liberal Party in London. After that headed up and grew a retail furniture company in NE England. Active in his trade association, played a lead role in the design of Flammability labels for sofas. A director of the British Shops and Stores Association and chair of a nationwide committee that set up the Qualitas Conciliation for the Furniture and Carpet Industry. Is, and has been for many years, chair of the board of a residential care home in Newcastle. Recently became chair of TYDFAS, the Newcastle branch of the National Association of Decorative and Fine Art Societies. A member of his local Rotary Club seeing this book and his involvement in Special Needs as acts of Rotary service.

Travels widely, enjoys music and the arts and is never, ever bored.

Were it not for Great Britain and those who sacrificed their lives against Nazism his life would have ended long ago in a gas chamber. Were it not for the medical profession and the NHS he would not be here today. Were it not for his teachers his life would not have been so rewarding. He sees this book as a way of expressing his thanks.

All of the Royalties from the book will go to the Community Foundation serving Tyne and Wear. The proceeds will assist children with special needs and to make contributions to Rotary Foundation, the Children's Foundation in the NE, the Jerusalem Foundation and to Neve Shalom, an interfaith community in Israel.

Printed in the United Kingdom
by Lightning Source UK Ltd.
125954UK00001B/214-270/A